My head was pounding like a sledgehammer against my chest. I looked away. My mind raced to come up with rationalization, but there was no way what I saw could compute.

I should have split, but my mind was boiling and I was getting angrier by the second. It was easy to sneak closer without being noticed, and I could hear every word they said . . .

When she said my name it was like I was in the electric chair and they'd just turned on the juice.

I took off—I'd heard enough. One thing I knew for sure, I had to get some distance on her real quick. I didn't want to look at her face.

CHANGES IN LATITUDES

WILL HOBBS

To Erin

Best Wishes

Will Hobbs

11·18·93

AN AVON FLARE BOOK

The author is grateful for permission to quote from the following songs:

"Changes in Latitudes, Changes in Attitudes" by Jimmy Buffett, © 1977 Outer Banks/Coral Reefer Music

"Wastin' Away Again in Margaritaville" by Jimmy Buffett, © 1977 Outer Banks/Coral Reefer Music

"Ripple": Words by Robert Hunter, music by Jerry Garcia; © 1971 Ice Nine Publishing Co., Inc.

"Throwin' Stones": Words by Bob Weir and John Barlow, music by Bob Weir; © 1984 Ice Nine Publishing Co., Inc.

AVON BOOKS
A division of
The Hearst Corporation
1350 Avenue of the Americas
New York, New York 10019

Copyright © 1988 by Will Hobbs
Published by arrangement with Atheneum Publishers, an imprint of Macmillan Publishing Company
Library of Congress Catalog Card Number: 87-17462
ISBN: 0-380-71619-4
RL: 6.1

First Avon Flare Printing: January 1993

AVON FLARE TRADEMARK REG. U.S. PAT. OFF. AND IN OTHER COUNTRIES, MARCA REGISTRADA, HECHO EN U.S.A.

Printed in the U.S.A.

RA 10 9 8 7 6 5 4 3 2 1

For my father
1915–1984

There is a road
No simple highway
Between the dawn
And the dark of night

And if you go
No one may follow
That path is for
Your steps alone

Robert Hunter

CHANGES IN LATITUDES

1

WE WERE LEAVING for a week in Mexico, all of us except my father, that is. For years he'd been putting down Mom's dream of vacationing in a tropical paradise, so she finally gave up on him and said we'd just go on our own. So here we are in the airport, milling around before the flight. Dad's in his jeans, and Mom's looking like she just walked out of a fashion magazine. Not exactly a matched pair. Jennifer and Teddy are sticking close together. Jennifer's fourteen, your standard kid sister. Attractive? Sure, but who'd say that about their sister? Teddy looks like a normal nine year old, but let me tell you something: he isn't.

I'm the one with the headphones and the shades, trailing behind like I'm only loosely affiliated with these people. I used to think I was the center of the universe, but by the end of the week down there I found out this wasn't the case. I found out something about what's really important and what's not. I guess that's why I'm writing this down, to let you know the price I paid and let you draw your own conclusions.

Back to the airport. Jennifer had just noticed some photographs of animals in a glassed-in display. Over the pictures it said in big letters, "THINK BEFORE YOU BUY." I wish she hadn't, but she pointed it out to Teddy. He was over there so fast he could've smashed his face.

He stood there staring with his mouth open. Over his shoulder I saw bloody elephants on their sides with their tusks sawed off, dead leopards, dead rhinoceroses, dead polar bears, dead whales, a mound of dead sea turtles, and on and on. I looked over to Teddy—he was horrified. I told you he wasn't a normal kid.

"Endangered feces," I said.

When he heard that blasphemy, Teddy glanced my way with a hurt and disbelieving look. Disbelieving, I don't know why—I did it to him all the time. "Lighten up," I told him.

Despite the one-sided evidence to the contrary, he wanted to believe that deep down I was as kind and idealistic as he was.

"Look at all those sea turtles," Dad said.

I wish my father hadn't done that. I don't think Teddy had registered on that particular photograph. Now that Dad pointed it out, he took a long look.

While they talked about whether there would be sea turtles on the Pacific coast of Mexico, I checked out examples of illegal items tourists try to bring back into the States, like ivory, furs, curved daggers with

4

hilts of rhino horn, even skin lotion made from turtles.

"Ever seen a bottled sea turtle?" I asked.

I wish I hadn't done that. Teddy came over and had another long look.

"Cut it out, Travis," my sister said. She harbored the suspicion that deep down I was truly twisted. She always was a better judge of character than Teddy.

My mother was getting bored, I could see, and was about to open her mouth and get us moving, so I launched into a reading of the display's big message in the same gloriously insincere style a game-show host uses to announce prizes:

> "If trends continue, within fifty years over half of the world's wild animal species will be extinct. The seemingly harmless purchase, in any quantity, of products derived from these animals can only hasten their decline. The Endangered Species Act makes it illegal for anyone to bring such products into the United States, for personal as well as commercial use."

"I can see this is going to take some time," my mother got in edgewise. "Travis, would you stay with Jennifer and Teddy please? We'll be over at the coffee shop. Your father and I need to talk before we go."

This was obviously news to Dad. She was still mad at him for not coming, I figured, and wanted to get off some parting shots. He went along without saying anything.

After awhile they were back and we lined up at the gate. Dad gave presents to everyone, mostly books. When he came to me he said, "Travis, you're the only one who doesn't get a book."

"That's okay," I said. "I can't read."

He grimaced. He hates it when I put myself down, even if I do it for the comedy. He even goes so far as to say I'm as smart as Teddy.

"Some tunes for your Walkman," he said, and handed me a cassette.

"It's dated," he half-apologized, "but for a trip to Mexico, it's essential."

"What kind of stuff?" I asked. We were all shuffling along, nearing the front of the line for boarding. The PA was announcing what we did and didn't need, birth certificates, tourist cards, whatever. All of a sudden I realized my father was all choked up and about to lose it.

But he kept talking. "Jimmy Buffett. You know, 'Changes in Latitudes, Changes in Attitudes.'"

I didn't know what to say. Suddenly, we were squeezing through a little checkpoint and my father stepped to the side. It was happening fast but it was an awkward moment that seemed to hang up in time and still does. I remember a little of what we were like. Teddy was spooked, very confused. Jennifer was sniffling. Mom was impatient. She'd told us she was determined to have a good time, and we should too, even though Dad had done his best to sabotage the trip by not going.

Dad leaned toward us and whispered hoarsely, "I want you to know I love all of you very much."

That was it. I was the last through the door out to the plane. At the last second I looked back toward my father, but he had already turned away. He had his head in his hands, and he was crying.

6

 2 ≈

I DON'T WANT YOU to get the idea I left for Mexico with a heavy heart. I had no use for whatever it was that was going on between my parents: I was psyched about the trip. I'd been dreaming up some juicy scenarios for months, and here I was in the air and on my way. Within a few minutes of takeoff I lapsed into my fantasy about how I was going to meet a beautiful stranger. She'd be on vacation too. It was a conviction of mine that beautiful women on vacation are more accessible than they are at home.

Across the aisle, Teddy was submerged in the book Dad gave him. Next to him Jennifer and my mother were going over the airport scene, the latest installment in the family soap opera, their favorite show. Mostly I tuned out under my headphones.

7

Somewhere over Mexico, Teddy woke me up all excited about something he'd discovered in his book. "There's a nesting beach of the Pacific ridley just a few miles from Punta Blanca!"

"Oh?"

"There's only a few nesting beaches along the whole Pacific Coast."

"I'm not surprised. It sounds like a pretty rare talent for a beach to have."

Jennifer and Mom hissed. "Nesting beach of the Pacific ridley," Jennifer insisted. "Don't you listen?"

I couldn't tell if Teddy was enjoying this or not. Mostly he liked it when I shoved sticks into his spokes. He was about to ask Mom something, but I intercepted him. "Don't tell me," I said. "I think I know this. The Pacific ridley is a seabird, a distant cousin of the blue-footed booby. It lays its eggs on a nesting beach because it's too lazy to make its own nest—right?"

"They're sea turtles," he explained, only a little amused. "Can we go to that beach?" he asked Mom urgently. "This is the time of year they're nesting."

My mother's the master of the non-answer, and she was never sure Teddy should be so hung up on animals. "Let's wait until we get there," she said.

3

HAVE YOU EVER taken a ride in a Mexican taxi? Well, it was a first for me, and I mean to tell you we got our money's worth.

The airport at Punta Blanca is twenty miles out from the city. When we reached the curb out front, somehow we were funneled into a van with a bunch of other gringos. We all sat there for about twenty minutes and felt real stupid, not knowing what was going on.

Fortunately, my mother couldn't handle the heat in there and decided we'd get our own taxi. As we got out, a Mexican guy tried to shoehorn us right back in.

"We go to all the hotels," he assured us. "No problem. We leave in just a minute."

We didn't know what to say. "Let's get our bags, Travis," Mom said.

"Taxi," I explained to the man in my best Spanish accent. "Taxi to the hotel." I don't know why I was talking like that. It seemed like the thing to do at the time.

He looked at us like we must be the stupidest people he ever met.

What really made his day was when I pulled our bags from the bottom of the pile in the back of the van, and most of the rest came with them.

Down the curb a little ways there were a number of taxis to choose from. The driver of the first one we came to was leaning against his taxi, a laid-back guy who wasn't hustling everyone who came by. "Sol Mar Hotel?" my mother inquired.

"*Sí*," he answered. "No problem."

He never said another word, all the way in to Punta Blanca.

Taxi Number 22, I think it was. Ask for Number 22 if you're ever down there—maybe it'll be the same guy. Sure, there's lots of good drivers down there, but I have a hunch he's the best. When he cleared the airport like a getaway man leaving the scene of a job, Mom was pleased with herself. "We won't have to spend all afternoon getting to our hotel," she said.

But right about then, as we slalomed on two wheels around the "*alto*" sign and onto the two-lane main road, our driver shifted into warp speed. There isn't an amusement park on earth with a ride that compares with his.

When you're in a Mexican cab, it's like being inside a Christmas tree. There's all these stickers and dimestore gadgets and little statues. It's gaudy enough, but you like it just the way it is because you realize it's all tied in to the driver's delicate psyche and has something to do with your survival. I got under the Walkman, slipped in my new tape, and turned the volume all the way up. That's what I would recommend as the best strategy for this trip—it worked for me. It takes care of the driver's horn for one thing. He's always leaning on it because he's so angry at whatever's slowing him down, like the car three feet in front of him. If you notice it at all, the horn fits right into Jimmy Buffett's music.

Sometimes music is made-to-order for the situation, as if it were written with you in mind. Check this out:

> It's these changes in latitudes, changes in attitudes,
> Nothing remains quite the same.
> With all of our cunning and all of our running,
> If we couldn't laugh we would all go insane.
> If we weren't all crazy we would go insane.

Teddy, Jennifer, and my mother didn't have the benefit of the Walkman, I'm afraid. The g-forces had me and Teddy and Jennifer plastered against the back seat, and they were terrified out of their minds. You've never done hairpin turns on a mountain road until you've done them with this guy. Mom had her hands braced against the dash and looked like she'd gone catatonic. I was playing air guitar along with the music, probably singing along, too. I thought it was all perfect and funny, including how scared they were. We were in Mexico, no doubt about it.

Actually the driver had it all under control, sort of. Cows appeared right in front of us and somehow he missed them. Every time it seemed we were sure to

11

fly off a cliff, he held the road by a fraction. One time, though, he pulled out to pass a truck loaded with watermelons, and there was this other taxi right there coming at us every bit as fast as we were at him. I knew for a fact I was going to die.

We didn't sneak back in behind the watermelons— no way. We went for it. Our driver's honor was at stake.

That other taxi driver wasn't slowing down either. Neither was the truck driver. Everybody's honor was at stake.

Well, I'm happy to tell you we passed that truck and slipped in barely ahead of him, maybe a tenth of a second before that other taxi came on through. No problem. A tenth of a second is just as clean a miss as three or four seconds, after all. That's why I have to admire our driver and why I'd recommend him to you. I'll bet he's as skillful as any fighter pilot in the United States Air Force.

After we came off the steepest part of the mountain I caught a view of the surf pounding in at the bottom of the cliffs. Then we came to a spot where you could see Punta Blanca to the south and I saw why people come there. Punta Blanca, shining white against steep green mountains and tucked in the arms of a big blue-green bay: the travel posters can't begin to do it justice. I pointed it out, and that brought the others around a little. My mother couldn't see it at first; probably she was seeing spots.

What sticks out when you first see Punta Blanca even from a distance are the high-rise hotels on the north end. "Look at the high rises!" Mom gushed. They're beautiful in their own way, I have to admit.

They say thirty years ago Punta Blanca was a sleepy fishing village. You always hear that expression, "sleepy fishing village." I picture peasants in serapes sleepwalking their way along the cobbled streets, the entire town afflicted with narcolepsy. Every now and then a drowsy fisherman takes his boat a little ways out into the bay, lowers his nets, and catches a few fish while he's dozing off. After awhile he goes home with his fish to his family, who wake up just enough to eat before it's time for siesta.

Aren't stereotypes wonderful? Mexicans like to sleep, Russians are warlike, the French are sexy. There must be something to it, because I saw all kinds of Mexicans sleeping in their hammocks in the middle of the afternoon. So I'm afraid of the Russians, and I'd really like to try France sometime.

A sleepy fishing village, as I was saying. Thirty years ago. Then an American film company lugged its equipment and people hundreds of miles over donkey trails and made a film there.

It must have been a pretty good film. The village grew into a town that spread around the bay and became a city, attaching itself even to the mountainsides—all with the speed of time-lapse photography. The people in the movie must have been having lots of fun, because tourists have been streaming down there ever since to get in on it.

I'll have to find out the name of that movie sometime and go see it. It'll be the most personally meaningful one I'll ever see. After all, we wouldn't have gone down there if they hadn't made that film in the first place. That's how fate works, isn't it? They could easily have botched it, made a movie nobody wanted to see. Or filmed it in black and white.

 4

As we reached the city's north end and drove right by the entrances to the big hotels, my mother was fairly drooling. She knew all about them from her guidebook. "There's the Sheraton," she cried. "There's the Las Palmas. There's the El Presidente!"

There must have been a dozen of them. It was hard to tell, we were going so fast. Then we sped through the narrow cobbled streets of the old part of town toward our own hotel, the Sol Mar, which Mom's guidebook described as "a good choice for the budget-minded."

One thing I saw right away: this end of town where we were going was Mexico, not a transplanted piece of America. The streets were narrow and packed with little shops and restaurants, and the Mexicans outnumbered the gringos two to one. I didn't know how I

15

felt about that. But then I sensed it was making my mother uncomfortable, and I started to get into it.

The Sol Mar turned out to be right at the beach and it didn't look half-bad. There were two wings, one along the beach and one facing the side street where we drove in. Four stories, hundreds of rooms, and every one had big sliding glass doors that opened out onto a balcony.

"*Cuánto?*" my mother asked the driver, blowing a quarter of her Spanish vocabulary.

"*Cuatro mil pesos,*" he answered.

Teddy, Jennifer, and I got out and stood around stretching and looking it all over. At the top of the stairs into the hotel, two guys in cheesy uniforms were checking us out.

"We survived," Jennifer said.

My mother fumbled in her purse and came up with four hundred pesos. I had a feeling that wasn't right, but I couldn't remember what *mil* meant.

Our driver shook his head with a big smile. He wasn't upset or anything. "*Cuatro mil,*" he repeated.

When he saw how confused Mom was, he wrote out the number *4000* for her on a slip of paper.

"How much is that, Travis? I can't think."

"Around twenty-five bucks."

She was sick, too stunned to close her mouth. The driver waited patiently. When he wasn't behind the wheel he was the most laid-back guy you'll ever meet.

My mother wasn't going to let him rip her off. She spied an older gringo couple coming out of the hotel and told me to go ask them what it should cost.

"Cuatro mil pesos," I told her when I returned. "Twenty-eight bucks." Then I added, just for fun, "Two dollars apiece if you take the van."

Meanwhile, the driver had taken our bags out of the trunk. I was watching Mom pay him off, and before I knew it the two guys in the cheesy uniforms had their hands on our luggage and were starting for the stairs. "Hey, hold on there Jackson—*no gracias!"* I yelled.

That got their attention. There was no way I was going to let them get away with carrying our bags thirty feet and get paid for it.

I couldn't recall the Spanish, so I pantomimed "we" and "carry." These guys looked at me like I was a complete fool, dusted off their tarnished dignity, and retired to the top of the steps.

As we took up our bags we were caught in the full bloom of Number 22's exhaust. He ought to have his catalytic converter and his pollution control valve looked at.

The lobby was practically empty. On the right was a long counter with three clerks behind it, two young men and a young woman. They didn't seem to see my mother at the desk holding her reservations in one hand, her phrase book in the other.

"Perdón—excuse me—*yo tengo una reservación por cuatro."*

They didn't pick up on that.

"What's 'today,' Travis? You took Spanish."

"Flunked it," I said cheerfully. "But I think it's *'hoy'*—something like that. Say *'para hoy'*—'for today.' "

"Yo tengo dos cuartos para hoy," she said.

17

One of the men looked at her and said in perfect English, "I'm sorry, but we don't have any rooms available."

"There must be some mistake," Mom told him. "We have two rooms reserved for five nights starting tonight and we already paid for the first two nights."

"Yes," he agreed, "but we don't have any rooms. When you get home you can get a refund through your travel agent."

"I can't believe this," Mom said. "We had a reservation—I'd like to see the manager."

"Sorry," the man told her. "I am the manager."

Dog-tired and demoralized, we retreated into the lobby. "What are we going to do now, Mom?" Teddy wondered in a shaky voice.

Right about then a young guy walked up to us. A gringo. He couldn't have been much older than me. He wore a blue T-shirt that said "Punta Tours" and had a leaping marlin on it. He had a mess of brochures in his hand.

"Excuse me," he said to Mom. "I think I can guess what happened to you up there. Maybe I can help."

She looked him over. Instinctively, she didn't like him. I think I felt the same way—I don't remember. There was something about him pretty flaky around the edges.

"You had a reservation," this guy went on, "probably paid in advance, and didn't get a room?"

"That's right," Mom said impatiently.

"Happens all the time down here."

She looked away from him and over to us and said, "Let's go find another place to stay."

"That's going to be hard to do," he said quickly. "They're usually all full. Of course, you could try the Strip."

"What's that?" I asked.

"The high-rise American hotels up the beach a few miles—you probably saw them on your way in. But they start at a hundred dollars a night."

"A hundred dollars?" Teddy said, big-eyed.

"Per room of course."

"So what are you suggesting?" Mom demanded.

"Just ask if there aren't some other rooms, if yours are full. Pull out twenty dollars while you're talking and say you wouldn't mind spending a little extra to get into something a little more expensive, because you really like the hotel."

"I'm catching on," Mom said wearily, and started off.

"What happens to people who don't get a room?" I asked him.

"They pound the pavement, maybe sleep back at the airport. Usually they find a place to stay the next morning. Sometimes they just go home."

While he was talking to me, he was checking out Jennifer.

"Do you live here or something?" I asked.

"I've been down here for . . . almost a year. I work for Punta Tours."

He handed Jennifer a brochure, gave her a smile. "We've got bus tours, fishing trips, snorkeling, diving. . . ."

"Sounds really good," she said brightly. "That's the kind of stuff we want to do."

19

Mom was back with keys, a whole lot happier. "Money talks!" she said.

"Got your rooms—good deal. Well . . . maybe I'll see you around. Name's Bill."

"Thanks a whole lot," my mother said. "We really appreciate it."

"Sure—glad I could help."

Pᴏᴏʀ Mᴏᴍ. When she turned the key and first entered her room, she stepped on a cockroach. It made the most exquisite crunching sound you can imagine. I had to crack up.

Poor Mom. A world-class beauty who could put the most splendid females in the jet set to shame, she somehow finds herself the mother of three, married to an unambitious, downwardly-mobile junior high school science teacher, and mired somewhere below the middle of the middle class. Her first-ever tropical vacation finds her herding her kids to Mexico on a budget. She'd like to be in the Greek islands gracing the deck of a yacht.

Teddy and I liked our room just fine. It was bright and spacious and we had it all to ourselves. From the balcony we looked out on the edge of town, the ocean, and the mountains. Quite a sight. Rock 'n' roll loud enough to energize the whole city poured out from under one of the palm-thatched roofs of the open-air huts they call "*palapas*" down on the beach. Imagine "Twist and Shout" in a Spanish accent. The funkiest aspect of our view was the block right across the street from us. Behind a stone wall a few families lived in small cinder-block houses and had a regular farm with gardens, papayas, and coconut palms, and chickens running around. Teddy really liked that. Dad would have liked it too. It would have made him feel more comfortable about being down there. I think he had the idea it was all going to be like the Strip.

We heard a shriek through the wall and I ran over to see if Mom or Jennifer had been savaged or something. It seems my mother got in on the last thirty seconds of hot water the Sol Mar was going to offer in the next week, and then found out about the normal state of affairs the hard way.

At breakfast the next morning the waiter brought Mom a note. She read it and tucked it in her purse. When Jennifer asked her what it was about, she said it was from the airline. Something about our flight back needed to be fixed up, and she'd take care of it during the morning.

We spread out our beach towels, all four of us, a little ways down from the hotel. Cooing over her baby, Mom lathered Teddy with sunscreen right away. "He's nine years old," I reminded her. "He can do that for himself."

She's quick. "I should have packed your swimming suit for you, Travis."

"You didn't bring much of one yourself," I said with a grin.

She just glared at me.

"What's wrong with cut-offs?" I snapped. "They're good enough for Dad."

She glared at me again.

"So, am I not supposed to mention his name? Is he dead, or what?"

Jennifer the peacemaker stepped between us right on cue. "Travis, please. . . ."

"Have you noticed any beachwear inspectors around here, Jennifer? I'm not the one making an issue out of nothing."

My mother heaved a sigh and smiled. "From what I've been told, they do have an attitude inspector. Fifteen years in a Mexican jail for bad attitude."

I like her when she's like that. She had me on the ropes.

"Let's all get along, Travis, please. Let's make this a perfect vacation."

Teddy's and Jennifer's eyes were saying the same thing.

"Hey, I'm cool," I said. "Pass the lotion—I'm thirsty."

After awhile my mother took off on her errand. Jennifer offered to go with her. "No," Mom said, "it might take all morning just to find the place. You guys enjoy yourselves. If you're not here I'll look for you in the hotel."

The beach was filling up. About half the people were Mexicans, mostly families with lots of kids running around screaming and playing soccer with their beach balls. Most of the gringos were over fifty. This scene wasn't exactly what I had in mind.

I asked Jennifer to stay with Teddy while I had a look around. She was on to me. "Cruising for foxes?" she teased.

I found one down at the very end of the beach, where the sand runs out as the bay turns a corner and the surf smashes into the rocks. She was lying on her back with her top off, erasing those unsightly tan lines. There was nobody down there but me and her, and she didn't know about me. I was close by in the rocks, as inconspicuous as the crabs.

She was a spectacular attraction. Punta Blanca should put her on the billboards.

I racked my brain for how I might approach her. "Great place, isn't it?" "Mind if I lie down?" "Can I help you with that lotion?"

Before I thought of the right line, she put on her top and left. But I was sold on Punta Blanca.

6

MOM'S ERRAND did take her all morning. Aero Mexico had discovered computers, she said, but not how to use them.

And I believed her. I didn't doubt for a minute that she had just spent the entire morning on a fool's errand. If we hadn't been in Mexico I might have suspected something sooner. But I was as naive as Teddy and Jennifer, enjoying my last hours of innocence.

In the afternoon I checked the end of the beach for my sunbather. Three times. Probably she'd left on an airplane.

With her gone I soured fast on our beach. In the evening, the rock 'n' roll started up again and I went down there to see what was happening, but I found out only the Mexicans went there at night. I stayed only long enough to verify that you can buy beer in Mexico without an I.D. It's good stuff, too.

The next morning found us on a walking tour of the old town, which Mom's guidebook described as an "absolute must" for local color.

I thought I'd hate it, but the guidebook was right. There's so much to look at, you see only a fraction of what's going on. A vendor offering all kinds of fruit I'd never even heard of peeled oranges, one after the other, with a razor-sharp knife the size of a machete. I tried one. It didn't taste anything like an American orange. Once you eat a Mexican orange, you realize that ours are victims of a conspiracy. Over the years, only the ones with less and less flavor have been allowed to reproduce, until there's no flavor at all.

Right next to the vendor there's a stand with dozens of whole chickens revolving on spits, and shish-kabobs of pork and beef. The locals are chowing down but you're not supposed to eat it. It looks great and smells so appetizing you can't stand it and have to move on.

But the bakery is two doors down. No American bakery smells that good. Come to think of it, nobody goes around smelling American bakeries.

We followed our noses inside. From a huge brick oven at the back of the shop a man was fishing out fresh loaves with a long-handled scoop. The guidebook says everything there is perfectly safe to eat. We went crazy, grabbed one of this and three of that, and ended up with two loaves of bread and at least a dozen rolls filled with jellied fruit. Everything was still warm. I handed the guy up front a thousand peso note. He gave me nine hundred and twenty back. All that for less than a dollar.

The indoor-outdoor cafes were everywhere. There was one right next to the bakery. We chose a table by the sidewalk and gorged on the pastries. Mom and I had coffee, so rich I have to wonder if the Latin American countries ship their used grounds north, and we're too stupid to figure it out.

We giggled and joked our way through the streets, actually having a good time together. Ordinarily I can't stand browsing in shops, but the colorful stuff they dangled out front lured me in behind the other three, and I was hooked. If I'd had the money I would have bought everything from the hand-woven rugs and the abalone-inlaid jewelry boxes to the ceramic birds and the onyx eggs. Everything in those shops was a work of art, even the junk.

At one of the shops Teddy tried out his Spanish and asked, "*Dónde esta tortugas?*" or "Where are the turtles?" A day had passed and he still didn't know where to find the nesting beach. The shopkeeper was confused for a moment, then sent his son out with some kind of instructions about *tortugas*.

A big stuffed sea turtle came through the door a few minutes later with a small boy's legs moving underneath. I was impressed—I didn't have any idea how beautiful they are. This one was gold and brown, with a streamlined, heart-shaped body, large front flippers, and head forward just like he was swimming. You'd never know his eyes were glass. Everything about him was smooth and clean and symmetrical. Whoever the taxidermist was, he did a great job.

As soon as I saw the turtle I started thinking, maybe I could chip in with some of my spending money and help Teddy out. The only problem would be, it's two feet long and maybe we couldn't get it home without breaking it.

But Teddy wasn't thinking about buying the thing at all. Wonder was written all over his face all right, but that quickly gave way to dismay as he said softly, "That was a hawksbill."

Then I remembered the display at the airport.

After the shopkeeper figured out he'd misguessed Teddy's request, he tried again, and directed our attention to a number of clear plastic bottles on the counter. They were filled with an off-white cream. "*Esta?*" he asked, handing me one. It had a picture of a sea turtle for its logo.

"It's very good for the skin," he said.

I could see Teddy was taking this personally, getting worked up about it.

"Ah . . . *muchas gracias,*" I told the man. *"Buenos días."*

"Lighten up," I told Teddy as we left. He wasn't saying anything and he looked pretty down-in-the-mouth.

In the next place we split up, and I found something I knew I had to have as soon as I laid eyes on it: a stuffed frog on a wooden pedestal, a huge stuffed frog standing on its hind legs and playing the bongo drums. When I saw it up close I realized it was a real frog—that's what made it so perfect. Somebody had actually skinned a bullfrog and stuffed him in this crack-up pose with the drums. I couldn't believe it. He was mine in a minute.

I found Teddy across the shop. He was tapping one of two middle-aged American women on the shoulder. They were standing by a pyramid of turtle lotion bottles on a counter.

"Excuse me," he said to the woman with several bottles in her hand. "You can't take that back to the United States."

She was sure surprised to hear something like that out of the mouth of a little kid. "Oh?" she said.

"Why not?" asked the second woman matter-of-factly, with a twinkle of amusement.

This was going to be too good to interrupt, so I hung back.

"Because it comes from an endangered species," Teddy said earnestly.

"Come to think of it. . . ." the second woman said.

"They'll take it away from you," Teddy added.

The first one was thinking fast. "We won't get one for Miriam, and we can use ours here."

Teddy was slow to react. He didn't know if he should let them off the hook or not. The first woman was hopeful, but then he spit it out. "You see, as long as people buy it they're going to keep making it."

That did it. The first woman leaned down and started getting loud. "Well, they sure don't seem to be endangered. This lotion is all over the place," she blathered, waving one of the bottles in his face, "and there's turtle soup and turtle steak in every restaurant!"

This outburst happened to fall on the ears of Mom and Jennifer, who'd just entered the shop. They appeared on the scene just as I had decided to make my move.

Mom made it for me. "Excuse me," she said, and pulled Teddy back.

"I can't believe this child is lecturing us about turtles," the first woman huffed.

"Well, I think he's right," her friend announced decisively. "We shouldn't buy it."

"Speak for yourself, Betty."

The two women left, upset with each other. But without any lotion, I might add.

My mother was agitated.

Jennifer admonished her little brother. "Teddy, you just can't . . ."

"I know," he blurted, "but they just don't know what they're doing!"

"That's exactly right," Jennifer told him. "They don't know what they're doing. It's not really their fault."

"How can anybody make that lotion?" Teddy cried.

I couldn't resist. "Easy," I said, "with a blender."

Predictably, none of the three enjoyed that remark. I became the villain of the piece, especially for watching it happen. None of them liked my frog, either. In fact, they hated it. It spooked Teddy, and Mom said it was macabre. Jennifer said it looked like it had something to do with voodoo, and termed it "definitionally gross."

I atoned for everything by volunteering to find the location of the nesting beach and lead Teddy there that very afternoon while Mom and Jennifer did some more browsing. Everyone was happy with that settlement, including me. I was ready to get on the road and have a look around.

7

I ASKED FOR the *playa* (beach) *de los huevos* (of the eggs) *de los tortugas* (of the turtles). It worked. The name of the nesting beach turned out to be simply Playa Tortugas.

Just a few blocks from our hotel we caught the bus marked "*Ruta 1.*" It was so packed I didn't think we'd be able to get on. That didn't turn out to be a problem. About fifteen people boarded after us.

With my face planted in a guy's back, I didn't catch many views. I know we climbed the spur of the mountain south of town, hugged the tops of the cliffs for a minute high above the sea, then switchbacked down to sea level again. We were there in a few minutes.

Playa Tortugas is no major attraction for either tourists or locals. One ramshackle cafe-*palapa* sits at the north end where we got off. Backed by groves of palms, the beach looked deserted and undeveloped for miles.

Teddy wanted to scour the beach for turtles, the sooner the better, but I insisted we visit the cafe first.

No more than a handful of people were there. With a breeze coming in off the ocean it was cool and comfortable under the thatched roof. We watched a woman barbeque whole fish on sticks and prepare side dishes on a propane stove. We started with an orange pop for Teddy and a *cerveza* for me, and then as we watched some other people eat we got brave and ordered meals for ourselves. We dug our toes into the sand and chowed down on fresh sea bass, rice, bread, and soup. Along with the meal each of us was served a plate of quartered limes, and we followed the lead of the Mexicans at the next table and squeezed them on and into everything, including my beer. The Latin music was blasting out of the radio and we were living it up.

As we ate we watched some kids running back and forth on the short pier down at the water, where a few beat-up motorboats were docked. Then they started playing in an odd, three-sided enclosure next to the pier. Made of poles planted close together, it extended from the beach into the water a good ways. The kids would run down the beach into the enclosure, yelling and screaming and having a great time.

After we finished our meal we walked out on the beach to see what was going on down there. The shrieking had really picked up. The kids seemed to be looking for something in the water, then running up the beach as soon as they'd found it.

We walked up close. They were standing knee-deep in the water, bending over and looking for something.

Suddenly, one of them lunged with his hands and came up with a lively three-foot shark. He lifted it high for a moment and made like he was going to throw it at the others, who kicked up a lot of water and got out of the way in a hurry.

After that they all ran off. I waded into the water to see if I could find the shark.

"Do you think it's safe?" Teddy worried.

"You stay back there. Here he is. There he goes. He ain't comin' on like Jaws. Hey, wait a minute—"

I'd seen something, a dark shape. I looked closer. Sure enough.

"What is it?" Teddy called.

"Come here."

He waded in. "I don't see anything."

"Right there, cheeseball," I yelled, and pointed at the sea turtle. Through two feet of water his dark back was camouflaged against the sand. He was about the size of a manhole cover.

Teddy's face lit up with pure happiness. He extended his hands, palms up, and we did a few quick high-fives. "All right!" he shouted. He looked at me like I'd given him the world.

"Sluggish dude," I said, nudging the turtle with my foot.

"That's probably because he—or she—is in captivity. They migrate all over the ocean."

"Let's bring him up on the beach where we can get a better look. Do these guys bite?"

"I don't think so . . . they're vegetarians. . . ."

I hauled him through the water toward the beach. "What do they eat?"

"Turtle grass."

"Makes sense."

I pulled him out of the water and up on the sand. It was a beauty—the most irresistible reptile I'd ever met, and Teddy had introduced me to hundreds. It started looking around and slowly digging into the sand with its flippers as if to turn around. "Just look at this scumbag!" I yelled.

Teddy knelt next to his prize, absorbed in turtle-worship. "It's a ridley—they call it the olive or Pacific ridley. The 'olive' is for the green color. It's the kind that lays its eggs here."

"Right around here, eh?"

"They always come back to the same beach to lay their eggs. Only the females go on land, and the only time they do is when they lay their eggs. This one's probably a female that got caught when it came ashore."

"If she had any sense she would walk right up the beach and around the poles, and get back in the ocean. Look, she keeps trying to go back in here."

"This doesn't look like a pen, but it is," he said sadly. "She probably already laid her eggs. She won't go onshore again."

That dulled my admiration. "Dumb," I said. "Can't even see her own situation when it's right in front of her face."

ORIGINALLY I'd hoped to check out the Strip in the afternoon, but that was already blown anyway. Half a mile down the Playa Tortugas we hadn't seen anything but sand and palm trees. The surf was gentle there, and I swam some while Teddy searched on down the beach for turtles. Then I got out and ran at angles in and out of the surf until I caught up with him at the high-tide mark. I told him it was time to be heading back.

"Just a little bit farther," he pleaded.

"You expect thousands of 'em to come out of the water and lay their eggs for you, right on cue?"

"It's the right time of the year. But I think they come ashore at night, according to the moon somehow. I'm looking for tracks but so far I haven't seen any."

I decided I wasn't in a hurry—he was having a good time. "How many does each one lay?"

"Eighty to a hundred, but hardly any survive because crabs and birds and fish eat 'em. They have lots of other enemies, too."

He knew his stuff. I'm sure he already knew by heart everything about reptiles in that book Dad gave him. Teddy had always been obsessed with animals, especially reptiles. By the time he was four he could make his own noose on the end of a long stem of wild oats, as Dad had shown him, and was catching his own lizards. He hated it when kids caught lizards by hand. Half the time they'd smash them, and nearly always the lizards would panic and snap off their tails trying to escape. Teddy would never keep one more than a few minutes, either. He always thought it was cruel to make any kind of wild creature live in captivity.

Turtles had always been his favorite reptiles. I remember the time Teddy found out about a pair of brothers who were keeping box turtles in their fenced backyard. These kids would go out in the woods and across the fields every day after school and search for box turtles. Eventually they'd collected over a dozen. Teddy knew all about it because the brothers rode on the same bus with him, and often they'd bring their turtles to school. Kids would paw them all day, and turn them on their backs over and over again just to see them right themselves.

Teddy got to where he wasn't thinking about anything else but those poor box turtles living in captivity. He was a mess. Finally, he decided something had to be done and he asked me to help him make a turtle-raid. I was amazed, but the idea really appealed to me, so that's what we did. We liberated sixteen box turtles from that yard and released them miles away. We never got caught, either.

Teddy, the child prodigy. I don't like to use the word "genius" because it makes him sound like an eggplant or something. As we walked along the Playa Tortugas I asked him why he liked sea turtles so much. His regard for them was on the highest plane I'd seen yet.

Suddenly he turned shy. "I dunno. . . ." he said awkwardly, and then added, "I just think they're really neat."

"You must be a reincarnated turtle or something."

He took that for a compliment and warmed up again. "Turtles were in the sea even before the dinosaurs disappeared," he explained. "And that was sixty-five million years ago."

"They do look ancient somehow."

"Man is only a few million years old."

This had possibilities. I told him, "I sure can't blame you for admiring turtles more than humans. They don't shoot guns and kill each other, for example."

He looked at me oddly. I don't think he'd ever thought about it this way, but he had to admit it was true. It had always been obvious that Teddy used his interest in natural science as a refuge from family conflict and human interaction in general.

"Turtles don't manufacture nuclear bombs," I continued. "Can't you picture a nuclear war with a turtle president pushing the button, turtle bomber pilots scrambling for their B-52s, and turtle submarine commanders saying 'You heard me, men—commence firing procedures.' "

Teddy's smile faded as my laughter took on a lunatic edge. I could tell he was worried about my mental health, a topic of occasional concern in my family.

"Can't you just picture Mom and Dad as turtles," I added as I was winding down, "hollering and breaking dishes?"

I looked up and saw two Mexican soldiers approaching with big rifles over their shoulders. Seemingly they'd come out of nowhere. They looked at me strangely—they must have heard me laughing. I straightened up in a hurry. I knew they could lock me up for smiling on a cloudy day if they felt like it.

Fortunately, the sun was shining. The soldiers passed on by and I was happy to proceed south and put some distance between us and them.

Ahead of us birds were circling and screaming. They were also diving to the beach. Teddy ran toward them as fast as he could. I caught up in time to see one of them fly off with what I took for a crab in its beak. "Get out of here, you dirtbags!" Teddy screamed. He was quite a sight, with his fists clenched and his white-blond hair waving, and fire in his eye.

Then I looked where Teddy was kneeling and saw perfect miniatures of sea turtles, dark little guys a couple inches long. They struggled jerkily along the sand with their flippers going, like windup toys.

"Far out," I marveled, and picked one up.

"Put him down! He's trying to get to the sea. You might mess him up!"

"Sorry," I said, and set him down. Like a dope, I'd set him in the wrong direction, but he turned himself around and took off as fast as he could. With the birds protesting overhead, I could see why he was in a hurry.

We found a trail of them coming from higher up on the beach and followed them back to the spot where they were popping out of the sand. Then we ran back to the waterline. Some were reaching the water and taking off, paddling like crazy. I could see what Teddy meant about their chances—it seemed like a mighty big ocean out there.

As long as we ran around and screamed at the birds they were afraid to dive. More of the hatchlings reached the surf and disappeared. What a feeling we shared, shepherding those baby turtles.

Wouldn't you know it, along comes a guy and starts picking up the hatchlings. We ran over to see what he was up to. He was putting them in an open Styrofoam cooler with a little water in it. He was a grubby-looking fellow, barefoot, kind of beaten-down, in soiled green trousers and a long-sleeved shirt. "*Qué pasa?*" I asked him.

He mumbled toothlessly in Spanish while he stooped and picked up more hatchlings. I couldn't understand a word he said. "*No comprendo,*" I told him.

He nabbed the last turtle—he'd collected about twenty—and pointed vaguely south down the beach. I could see a couple of long metal buildings way down there in the palms.

From his shirt pocket he produced a smudged business card. It read:

LABORATORIO SALAZAR
"para la mejoría de la reproducción de tortugas"

"What's that mean?" Teddy asked.

"A laboratory for the something of the reproduction of *tortugas*," I told him.

The Mexican took off with his turtles in the direction of the metal buildings.

"Maybe they're saving them from the birds," Teddy ventured.

"So why'd he have to pick 'em up and take 'em away?"

"It doesn't make any sense. Let's follow him."

The buildings were a long ways down there. "We gotta get back for dinner," I told him. "How'd you know what those birds were doing, anyway?"

"I saw it once on a show. Those were frigate birds."

The way he said it, "frig-it," you knew they were the scum of the bird kingdom.

"Frig the frig-it birds," I said. "I'm hungry."

# 9

MOM'S REALLY thinking about getting a divorce," Jennifer told me as we walked along the beach in front of the Sol Mar. When Teddy and I got back, she said we had to talk. Mom was going to take us out to a big dinner and show called the "Fiesta," but we didn't have to leave for another hour.

"So what else is new?" I said.

"This is different, Travis."

I knew right away it was. Jennifer's so easy to read, and she doesn't get this worried unless there's a four-alarm fire in progress. She's so calm and stable, sometimes I wonder how she got into this outfit. She's the family counselor. Early on she figured out it was her job to keep the family together.

"It has something to do with what happened at the airport, doesn't it?" I said. "What did she tell him?"

"She didn't say—she didn't talk about that. But I'm afraid you're right."

"Right about what?"

"That it has something to do with back at the airport."

"Tell me what she told you this afternoon."

"Mom was moody. You know how she can get really depressed. I asked her if she was mad at Dad for not coming."

"Yeah? What'd she say?"

"She said she knew he probably wouldn't come. I told her, 'It's not like he's out having a good time—he's always working.' "

"Right on. He's banging nails during his vacation to pay for our trip."

I realized when I said it, it wasn't that simple. I knew full well he never really wanted to come, as Mom had claimed. The idea of vacationing in a Third World country made him really uncomfortable. Something about the morality of it all. "What'd she say about him always working?" I asked.

"Mom said, 'That's just it. He's always working, and we're barely paying the bills. We don't have time, we don't have money, we're missing out on all kinds of opportunities. . . .' "

"That's a dead horse—what else?"

"She said it might have been different if he'd had a decent profession in the first place."

"She's never been jazzed about him being a teacher."

Jennifer shook her head. "Did you ever hear her talk like that—'it might have been different'? She said a lot more."

"Like what?"

"When I told her my friends say Dad's the best teacher

42

they ever had, she said something like, 'Nobody cares if you're killing yourself for their kids, and he'll never get paid well, no matter how much education he has or what a great job he's doing.' She said teachers were 'victims'—she was pretty bitter. Anybody with any sense or imagination gets out of it, she said, or they never get into it in the first place. Then she said, 'With his mind, he could have done anything. All his carpentry does, and my working, is subsidize his teaching job.'"

I had to think about that. I'd never heard her spell it out like that.

"I told her we do all right," Jennifer continued. Tears gathered in her eyes. "Mom said, 'That's about all. We could have had more time for each other, lived in a better home, traveled. . . .'"

Jennifer looked me in the eye. She was trembling. "It's the way she said it, Travis."

"Well, did she actually say they're getting a divorce?"

"No. That's what was scary. I'm afraid she told Dad something at the airport. I'm afraid she's already made up her mind."

"C'mon, Jennifer. You're blowing this all out of proportion. How many times have you heard all this about what a great life she could be having if Dad weren't so boring, and how she doesn't want to be a middle-aged backpacker? This is all old news. She wouldn't know what to do with herself without Dad. Just let her talk—she loves to be melodramatic. Don't let it get to you."

"Well, I asked her if she still loved Dad. She didn't answer for a long time, and then she said, 'I don't know.'"

"Anything else?"

"She said, 'I only have one life, and sometimes I feel like it's going down the drain.'"

"Barf."

"I told her she has us, and we all have each other, and she couldn't have everything just exactly perfect."

"What'd she say about that?"

"She didn't say anything—she just stared off. After a minute, she apologized for thinking out loud. She said the important thing was to have a good time on our trip, and she was going to be a lot more cheerful."

"Well, so what's the problem?"

"We have to do something, Travis."

"Like what?"

She hesitated, then spit it out. "Maybe if she could really relax down here, she could go back with a better outlook. She'd see that things aren't really so bad, and that her family is really important to her, and that we can really have a great time together."

"And that's why you told me all this, right? You think I'm going to prevent us from having a nice time."

She was scared, and she was asking "pretty please." I made a magnanimous gesture. I told her I'd take it under consideration.

 10 ≈

MY MOTHER LIKED IT, but if you ask me, the Fiesta was a bust. Hundreds of gringos pack the place every night and lay out big bucks for TV-dinner Mexican food and canned entertainment. You're mouthing a cold burrito, trying not to gag, and a mariachi band moves in and croons in your face. They hover there with their gaudy outfits, outsized mustaches, and flashing teeth, looking just the way the gringos expect them to look and singing everything the gringos expect to hear.

Believe it or not, the climax of the evening's entertainment was cockfighting. Teddy had the right idea—he wanted to leave as soon as it started. But Mom had just ordered another margarita and told him we should respect cultural differences. I got to suspecting it was bloodthirsty gringos like the cheering crowd at the Fiesta who perpetuate cockfighting, but I didn't say a thing. I was trying not to upset anybody.

It was Teddy who said what I was thinking: "Dad wouldn't like this."

To which Mom replied: "Darling, your father isn't here."

Probably it was the margarita, but she might have had another motive for staying. She always was worried that her blue-eyed boy was overly sensitive about cruelty to animals. Maybe she thought the cockfights would help desensitize him. Teddy just put his head down.

On the way home all of us were feeling sleazy. Mom said she hadn't known how awful it would be, that Teddy was right, we should have left.

Teddy saw an opening and asked if he and I couldn't return to the Playa Tortugas that night, since the moon was up and there was a chance a new wave of turtles might be coming in to lay their eggs.

There was no way we were going to go out on a beach at night, she said. She wanted us to get rested up for a day exploring the beaches at the Strip. She thought Jennifer and I might like to try para-sailing up there.

I didn't have to be sold on the idea. To Teddy's dismay I signed right up. I'd spent most of a day with him looking for turtles and now I was ready to cruise for foxes. I had my own goals.

Very early the next morning I was lying in bed thinking about what the Strip was going to be like. It wasn't light yet, but the roosters across the street thought it was time to wake everybody anyway. I heard someone trying a key in the door, and then the door slowly opened and slowly closed again with barely a sound. My heart went berserk. I knew someone was in the room, but a minute went by before I heard another step. I didn't know what to do so I sat up and switched on the light. And there was Teddy, tiptoeing around the side of his bed as sneaky as you please.

When the light came on he was as surprised as I was. "What do you think you're doing?" I demanded.

He didn't say anything—he was too busy trying to think.

His jeans were damp and covered with sand from the knees down, and sand was caked in the laces of his sneakers. "Better tell me," I warned.

He saw he didn't have any other choice. "I went to the Playa Tortugas."

It didn't seem possible, but I could tell he wasn't lying.

"Don't tell Mom," he pleaded.

"How'd you get there?"

"I walked. It doesn't take that long. The moon was out—it was easy."

That blew me away. My little brother was at least as sneaky as me. "Well, did you see any turtles?"

His face lit up. "I saw two! The first one was just coming out of the water. I watched her go up the beach, dig a nest with her back flippers, and lay her eggs. It was incredible! I was right there next to her and it didn't bother her a bit. It was like she was in a trance."

So was Teddy, telling me about it. He was still so high it was like he'd just been out flying without any wings.

"The other turtle I saw was being tagged by an American marine biologist. His name's Casey. You'd really like him, Travis. He told me that ten years ago, the whole beach would get so crowded with turtles during the arrivals that you could hardly walk through. And I only saw two!"

"What'd he think about seeing you out there?"

"He . . . told me I shouldn't be out by myself, and to watch out for poachers on my way back."

"Poachers? What do these poachers poach?"

"The eggs!" he cried indignantly, as his face flushed.

"Aha," I said. "They must be mighty good. I wonder why they poach them, though."

"I'm going to ask Casey that the next time I see him."

"Ask him if they don't ever scramble 'em."

He looked at me like, "How can you joke at a time like this?" He said, "They're stealing the eggs, Travis! I saw some men digging on my way back!"

"And there's nothing you can do about it."

He was really worked up. "I just can't believe they're stealing the eggs!"

"Sounds typical to me—par for the planet."

"I have to tell Casey."

"Well, don't forget we're going to the Strip today. Now how about getting some sleep?"

"I can't. I'm too excited."

"Do it anyway, cheeseball, or I'll bust you. And quit sneaking off without telling me what you're doing."

WE SET UP under one of the small *palapas* on the beach in front of the Tropicana. We just moved right in and nobody hassled us. Mom had read in her guidebook that the hotels don't own the beaches. They're all public so you can go wherever you please. My father would've liked that. He's a socialist at heart.

I was ready to cruise, so I didn't stay long. Jennifer, I could tell, was put out with me and Mom. She'd been lobbying for tours and trips advertised in the brochure she got from that fellow Bill the first night. She was graceful in defeat, I'll have to say. As I took off she was starting the book Dad gave her at the airport. Mom was marveling how Teddy had fallen asleep as soon as he lay down. I didn't say a thing. I grabbed my Walkman and I was gone.

It was late morning in paradise, and for two miles in front of those high-rise hotels, the beaches were packed with beautiful females sunning themselves like seals. I weaved in and out among them angling for views while I listened to Dad's tape. Right on cue, Jimmy Buffett was doing "Margaritaville." I knew this must be the place:

> Nibblin' on spongecake, watchin' the sun bake
> All of those tourists covered with oil. . . .

I found an especially attractive "seal" high up the beach and all by her lonesome. She was sunbathing on her stomach with her top unhooked, and there wasn't anyone within fifty feet of her. I spread out my towel and seated myself on her blind side where I could see to best advantage.

Then she turned her head toward me and saw me there hiding behind the sunglasses and trying to act disinterested. She hitched at her top. I lay down and turned my head away to show how disinterested I was.

The next time I looked she was shooing a fly, and she opened an eye to see if I was still there. She had me pretty well nailed so I got up and pretended I was leaving. I made a big arc and came up on her other side, quietly spread out my towel, and lay down even closer than before. There's something about that atmosphere around the Strip. The scent of her coconut oil went straight to my head and I felt like anything was possible. I got to wishing I'd lay down right next to her. I could reach out and touch her, and maybe. . . .

The heat must have been frying my brain. When she turned my way and saw me right there, she said real sarcastically, "Do you mind? . . ."

So much for my theory about beautiful women on vacation.

About an hour later I met a girl my own age. She was falling gently out of the sky underneath a bright red para-sail, and heading right for the spot on the beach where Jennifer and I stood. From my vantage point, she looked like a special delivery package from the gods.

The two Mexican guys working the landings and takeoffs didn't mind unharnessing her one bit—they had their hands all over her.

She didn't care; she had her motor running. She was whooping and carrying on about her flight. The contact high rippled right through me and on to all the people looking on. I was right there as she was getting unbuckled, looking pretty enthusiastic I suppose. The guy working on her said to me, "You'd like to try next, no?"

Not at the moment I didn't—I would have lost track of her.

She reached out and put her hand on my arm. "Hey, give it a try! It's fantastic! I guarantee it!"

I wouldn't have refused her a thing. I liked the way she moved in on me and made herself at home. Those guys should have signed her up to work for them. She could have sold me sand at a hundred dollars a pound.

I heard her yell "All right!" as the motorboat driver gunned it and I felt a huge lift. The sail took me up in a sudden rush to about the ten-story level on the high rises.

And what a rush it was, flying with that warm and humid tropical wind in my hair, taking it all in: fishing boats a few miles out, tourists on a ferry tossing food to hundreds of following gulls, swells coming in off

51

the ocean, thousands of colorful people on the beaches, the sleek and shining hotels with couples here and there having drinks on their balconies, all of Punta Blanca pulsing with music and light and color. But the best part was returning for a landing and seeing the girl still down there. She was talking with Jennifer and waving to me, and she had a big smile on her face.

We got a little acquainted while Jennifer was parasailing. Her name was Melissa and she was there with her father. Unfortunately, she was supposed to meet him for lunch and she was already late. She took off before I could ask where she was staying or anything. I did manage to ask her if she'd be back the next day. "Sure," she said.

"About the same time?" I yelled.

"Earlier," she called.

And that was that.

When we rejoined Mom and Teddy, Jennifer made a fuss about how I'd met a girl. It's hard to maintain your dignity when your sister considers your personal life family business. She's under the impression it's all healthy and normal and therefore discussable, the same as the price of groceries. If she could read my mind she wouldn't think that.

"She really liked Travis," Jennifer said, both to my mother and to me. I didn't mind hearing that.

"Sounds great," Mom said.

I thought I might as well tell them about my plans so they wouldn't come up with something else. I emphasized how we'd have to get an earlier start the next day. Mom said she'd be plenty happy to spend another day at the Strip. Jennifer didn't object. She liked the idea of me seeing Melissa again and she wanted to do some more para-sailing anyway. Teddy looked miserable.

My mother was dying to make the rounds of the shops in and around the hotels. She halfheartedly invited me, but I told her I already had my frog, so no thanks. After arranging a rendezvous with me, she and Jennifer left with Teddy in reluctant tow. I waited about two minutes, then slipped in the back way into the Tropicana. I was pretty curious about the hotels myself.

No, I'm not going to attempt to retrace all my movements of that afternoon. Probably I logged fifteen miles inside eight or ten hotels. Let's just say I rode dozens of elevators, prowled hundreds of hallways, poked into linen closets, hung around swimming pools, gawked at the casually elegant lobbies, and tried to educate a parrot.

All he could say was "Why not?"—not a very colorful mantra for a parrot. I repeated "You scumbag" for him a couple hundred times, but he just kept saying "Why not?" He was fixated on it. And why not? The more I thought about it, the more I thought he had something really profound there.

It might seem an odd time to have been thinking about my future, but that's what I got to daydreaming about as I prowled around the hotels soaking up the atmosphere. It wouldn't be that long before I'd be on my own, I thought. If I could figure out how to make megabucks, I could afford to spend six months of the year in places like this or even better, all over the world. Everyone knows that the most beautiful women on earth are attracted to good-looking men with lots of money who'll take them places, so why not oblige them?

I startled myself with the realization that my head was in the same place as my mother's, namely, that you were a dope if you weren't going after the good life. I'd always suspected that she was right, but now I was convinced. What was so wrong about staying in the best hotels and eating lobster dinners? The guests at the high rises didn't look any different from us— they just had more money. And what was so bad about that?

My father believes that you can't make a lot of money without exploiting people somehow, or exploiting the earth. He likes to repeat the statistic that an American uses fifty times more of the planet's resources in his lifetime than does a person born in the Third World. He believes in living simply. Though he's not religious exactly, he says it's harder for a rich man to get into heaven than it is for a camel to pass through the eye of a needle.

Apparently no one vacationing in Punta Blanca had heard the news. They all seemed to be having a good time, and it didn't seem to be all that awful. My father had really boxed himself in, I got to thinking. My mother was right. What good does it do, really, to go around worrying about people starving in Ethiopia, or the vanishing habitat of the mountain gorilla?

As I cruised those carpeted halls, peeking into doorways and hungering to throw myself into the lap of luxury, this is what I decided, despite the years of antagonism between my mother and me: if she was really thinking about getting a divorce, maybe it was more Dad's fault than hers.

I HUNG AROUND the para-sailing all too long the next morning. The girl never showed up. I wasn't pleased. I felt like kicking somebody.

When I came in sight of the *palapa* where I'd left the others, I saw Jennifer talking with a guy. Teddy was there but my mother wasn't around. As I arrived, the guy had just left and Jennifer was watching him go. Teddy looked up from his nature book, but when he saw me come in all bent out of shape he put his face back in it.

"Who was that?" I snapped.

"Bill," Jennifer said. "You remember, he helped us the first day."

"What'd he want?"

"He was just being friendly," she said defensively. She could tell my mind parasites were pretty active.

"Oh yeah? Did he ask you out?"

"As a matter-of-fact, he did. He wanted to show me around on his motorbike."

I didn't like the sound of that. No matter what you're up to yourself, your sister is another matter.

"Show you around, eh? What'd you tell him?"

"I told him I had to stay with Teddy."

"He's too old for you."

"He said we could go some other time."

"Forget it."

"Says who?"

"Are you going to see this guy, or what?"

She was pretty mad at me for bossing her. She raised her voice, which she doesn't do that often. "Look! You don't have to tell me what to do, Travis. I'm not sure I like him anyway."

I took that as a concession statement. I caught my breath and looked around. Teddy was still hiding under his book. Jennifer reached for the novel Dad gave her. "Where's Mom?" I demanded.

"She said she had some arrangements to check up on."

"What arrangements?"

"The flight back, I guess. I don't think she trusts the Mexican airlines."

"When's she getting back?"

"She didn't say."

"Well I'm splitting," I said, and took off. I wasn't in any mood to see my mother either.

13

GOT A GREAT TIP from a guy selling fish on a stick. Hermosa Beach, the one where they made the movie, was just a few miles north of the Strip. "All the beautiful people go there" was what he said. I hopped a bus and was there in a few minutes.

I wish I'd never run into that guy with the fish.

I wish the bus had broken down.

I wouldn't even have been out cruising if the girl had showed up for para-sailing like she said. Or if I'd been struck down by "Montezuma's Revenge" and had to stay at the Sol Mar.

Or if we'd never gone to Mexico.

Or if my parents had never met.

Of if an asteroid about five miles in diameter hadn't struck the earth at some precise moment in time sixty-five million years ago. That asteroid's collision with the earth, scientists theorize, packed a punch equivalent to that of a global thermonuclear war. So much dust was kicked up into the atmosphere and blocked the sun so effectively that the temperature never got above freezing for ten years.

Teddy was really big on the theory about the asteroid and the dinosaurs. If it weren't for that exquisite bit of timing, according to Teddy, none of us would be here today. Dinosaurs would have remained the darlings of evolution, and mammals would likely still be scurrying around underfoot trying to get out of the way.

Just think. If the asteroid had missed, which should have been millions of times more likely, some male adolescent dinosaur instead of me might have been staring down this white sand beach, and what he would have seen would have been a frighteningly familiar mother dinosaur massaging some stranger's shoulders.

Maybe I could come up with a couple dozen more "what if's," but I suppose I might as well get on with it. So here goes.

There she was, under a *palapa* down in a little grove of palms. I blinked to see if it could possibly be my mother. It really was. I thought I was savvy in the ways of the world, but I couldn't have been more surprised if my father had suddenly stuck a knife in my gut.

My heart was pounding like a sledgehammer against my chest. I looked away. My mind raced to come up with a rationalization, but there was no way what I saw could compute.

I should have split, but my mind was boiling and I

was getting angrier by the second. I couldn't simply leave and let her off the hook and never know—I had to know what this was all about. Had she just met this guy or what?

It was easy to sneak closer without being noticed. They were totally absorbed with each other. Concealed by the thatched shade behind them, I could hear every word they said. "You'd love the Caribbean," this guy was telling her. "We could really take our time and sail around the islands. St. John, St. Thomas, Guadeloupe, Martinique, Barbados, the Caymans . . . the scuba diving in the Caymans is unbelievable."

"Let's think about tomorrow first, Mitch," my mother said. "I'm not sure about tomorrow."

Her voice seemed melancholy.

"I'd have the car rented and ready to go. Just meet me at the Sheraton again."

"I hate to leave them alone."

"Is anything wrong?"

"No, but . . ."

"You'll only be gone a few hours."

"I worry about Teddy."

Then there was a pause. I didn't want to look through the thatch. She'd been sneaking off on us and was having an affair. Suddenly I smelled an acrid odor. It was me—I'd broken out into a stink like I've never smelled before. You'll recognize it if it happens to you.

"What about custody, Mitch? I've got to end up with Teddy. You know how precious he is to me."

"Sure."

"—and Jennifer."

I couldn't believe this. I just couldn't believe this.

59

"You got it, Linda. I have a friend who's the best custody lawyer I ever heard of."

"Travis would want to stay with his father."

When she said my name it was like I was in the electric chair and they'd just turned on the juice.

"And he's a pain, right?"

"Oh no, he's just very . . . complex."

"Sure."

"I really love him, Mitch. He . . . he wouldn't want to stay with me anyway."

I took off—I'd heard enough. I headed back for Jennifer and Teddy, seeing black and putting a few things together. Like all the bogus trouble with the airline tickets. When she was gone the first morning she was with him. That note she got from the waiter was from him. She was going to split again and they were going to go somewhere in a car. This whole vacation was phony—she knew this guy from home, and I don't suppose he just showed up. She rigged it so Dad wouldn't come so she could meet this guy down here. How much did Dad know, and what was the scene at the airport all about?

One thing I knew for sure, I had to get some distance on her real quick. I didn't want to look at her face.

My arrival back on our beach must have made my earlier one seem cheerful by comparison. They were both in chaise longues, reading. Jennifer looked up and said, "You're back."

"Let's go, Teddy," I growled.

"Where to?" he asked uncertainly.

"Don't you want to go back to your 'Turtle Beach'?"

He looked back and forth between me and Jennifer.

60

"Let's get out of here," I said.

"What about me?" Jennifer insisted. "How come I can't go? Anyway, you have to wait for Mom."

"That's where you come in."

"You can't just take off without checking with Mom."

"Watch me. Let's go, Teddy."

Teddy got up to come with me. Jennifer warned, "Ted–dy . . ."

"If Travis says it's okay . . ."

"Let's go, Paco."

"What do I say to Mom?"

We were already on our way. I stopped, turned, and looked at her. She was pretty upset. I had succeeded in spreading the misery around. "Just tell her where we went. She can always come down there if she wants. But I doubt if she can work it in to her *schedule*." I turned heel and took off with Teddy.

"Just because Melissa didn't show up," she called, "you don't have to take it out on everybody else!"

≈14

TU MADRE." That's a Spanish expression, one of the worst insults there is. It translates as "your mother."

It came to mind as I brooded over a Tecate in the cafe-*palapa* at the Playa Tortugas. I'd never properly appreciated that expression. Now I could. If someone had walked up to me right then at the beach and said that to me, I would have ripped his lungs out and then agreed with him.

I really wanted to rip somebody's lungs out.

Teddy kept looking over to the next table at a big, muscular, blond-haired gringo hunched over a Spanish-language newspaper. He was munching *empanadas* and drinking a *cerveza* as he read. Finally he looked up, and when he saw Teddy his face broke out in a smile as golden as Robert Redford's.

"Say, how's it going?" he said. "Teddy—right?"

Teddy nodded, and told me enthusiastically, "Casey's the marine biologist I told you about."

He didn't look like a marine biologist to me. In his muscle shirt, swimming suit, and thongs he looked more like a surfer. Or considering the tattoo on his arm and the three-day beard, like a biker.

"This is my big brother Travis," Teddy announced proudly.

"Glad to meet you, Travis," he said with that smile.

As savage as I felt, the smile disarmed me. There wasn't anything phony about it, maybe because of his eyes. There was a lot of mileage around his eyes.

"Your brother really knows a few things," he told me. "How 'bout you—are you interested in marine biology too?"

Though it had never occurred to me before, I told him I was. "I don't know much," I said, "but Teddy's been getting me into it."

Teddy was surprised and pleased, I could see that. I was surprised myself. I'd never heard myself say anything like that before.

Casey smiled. "How'd you guys like to go offshore and see if we can locate some turtles?"

A few minutes later we were in Casey's motorboat, picking up speed and heading out to sea. Teddy and I sat on the front thwart and helped weight the bobbing bow as Casey opened it up full throttle and really gave us a ride. Teddy was grinning like a mule eating briars. I glanced back to Casey. He nodded to me and broke into that smile, as if to say, "This ain't bad, eh?" It seemed as if the three of us had been together for years.

When we were a good mile offshore, three other small

boats appeared at a distance. Casey eased up some and steered in a big arc away from them.

"What are they doing?" Teddy asked.

"They're . . . fishing," Casey said. "We should do okay over this way."

Casey cut his speed, shaded his eyes, and started searching the water for turtles. We did the same, though I couldn't keep it up after a few minutes. Finally, Teddy saw one and cried out. It was paddling around just below the surface. We had no idea what Casey had in store for us. He fished two sets of snorkeling gear—masks, snorkels, and flippers—out of the rear thwart, coached us, and sent us after the turtles. "They mass offshore, the males and females both, well before the arrivals. Maybe we'll get lucky and you'll see some more."

We got the hang of swimming at the surface and breathing through our snorkels while we kept our faces down and scanned for turtles. Then we practiced diving until we could stay down a minute or two. After a number of dives I'd convinced myself we wouldn't see any, but then like an image in a dream they appeared in front of us, six of Teddy's olive-green ridleys swimming silently and effortlessly along, and we were right among them.

With the flippers we had no problem keeping up. Strangely enough, they showed no fear of us. I'm sure they could have sped up, or dived deep where we couldn't follow, but they held their own course. I felt like we were of the moment, and they were of the ages.

When we couldn't stay down any longer, we surfaced with a shout and let Casey know we'd found them.

He called his encouragement and we dived again. We hadn't lost them. This time we took hold of two of them, and let them lead us around. If we kept kicking we didn't hold them back. Then we let go and swam alongside them again. It didn't seem right to hinder their graceful movements—just to be there with them in their own element was enough.

For the first time in my life I was filled with awe. I was overwhelmed with the kind of appreciation for them that Teddy must have felt. As beautiful and perfect as wild geese, they swam like birds of the sea. Just as birds had mastered flight, these turtles were reptiles who'd taken to the open sea. If anything, they were more graceful than birds because the water slowed their movement to the speed of a hypnotic dance. It seemed a pity that they ever needed to return to the land to lay their eggs. Creatures of freedom and flight in the sea, they became awkward and hapless once they climbed out onto the beach.

Without realizing it, I'd started daydreaming the daydreams of a marine biologist.

For me that swim was a waking dream wrapped around and around with beauty. I was sharing it with my brother, and I was happier than I'd ever been. We'd left the land and the weight of our troubles behind, and for a short while in another dimension we experienced together the weightlessness of pure joy.

There's a place where that swim keeps on happening forever. That place is in my memory. I go there often. Teddy and I are swimming along with the turtles and looking to each other to share the wonder. We're the brothers we always wanted to be.

≈15≈≈≈≈≈≈≈≈

ON THE WAY in, Casey drove very slowly. None of us, it seemed, was in a hurry to get back to shore.

At one point Casey cut the motor back to idle and pointed out two turtles for us, right together. "There's a sight you don't see every day," he said.

Sure enough, they were stuck together.

"They're mating!" Teddy cried. "How long do they stay attached?"

"For hours sometimes," Casey replied. "Unfortunately . . ."

He was wondering if he should say what he was about to say. It seemed like he took a good look at Teddy and decided it was all right.

"Unfortunately that's one of the main reasons poachers steal the eggs."

"I forgot to tell you," Teddy interrupted excitedly, "—those eggs I saw being laid—they were dug up!"

Casey shook his head. "I'm not surprised."

"What's the story with the eggs?" I asked.

Again he seemed reluctant. "Ignorance," he said finally. "They're believed to be . . . an aphrodisiac."

"What's an aph-ro-di-si-ac?" asked Teddy.

"Cheeseball," I jeered. "He's talking about those two turtles. See if you can figure it out."

Casey wasn't too pleased with me, I could see, but he didn't say anything. "Drinking the raw eggs is thought to make a man more of a man. Beliefs like that are ancient, Teddy. It's similar to the way hunters in primitive cultures all over the world have always tried to acquire the characteristics of the prey they admired most, such as courage and strength and cunning."

"Yeah, like cannibals," I said for a laugh.

"That's exactly right," Casey said.

He dropped us off back where we started, at the short pier at the north end of the Playa Tortugas. We thanked him and were saying good-bye as he was about to take off in his boat. I wasn't sure I would see him again. "So what does it take to become a marine biologist?" I asked.

"About six years of college, if that's what you mean. At least your Bachelor's and Master's degrees."

"You probably have to have pretty good grades."

Casey nodded. I could see Teddy looking up at me like a miracle was happening or something.

"I could do that if I wanted to." As lame as it sounds, that's what I said.

Casey flashed that golden smile and looked right through me, and he said, "Maybe you will, Travis."

Then he drove out as we waved from the dock. "Take care, guys," he called.

Teddy turned to me all fired up. "You might be a marine biologist! We could be a team!"

"It's just a wild idea," I said. "But don't tell Mom or Jennifer anyway—or even Dad."

I didn't want to hear any more about that. "I could use a brewski," I said. "Why don't we cruise the rest of the beach?"

"We don't have to go back?"

The Hermosa Beach scene and the imminent disintegration of our family, the whole sleazy mess, came flooding back into my mind. "What for?" I said, with extra-thick sarcasm. I knew we'd get back late, but I couldn't have cared less.

I picked up a Tecate, Teddy got an orange *refresco*, and we headed down the beach. We played tag some with the waves, and I remember Teddy pointing out frigate birds, but mostly I was preoccupied as I went over a few things in my mind. Like who this "Mitch" was that my mother was with. If she picked Dad out for his looks, she wasn't going to make that mistake again. It wasn't hard to guess what she saw in the new model—undoubtedly he had megabucks.

And they were going to get married. Not only that, they were going to take Teddy and Jennifer with them. Here I'd been telling Jennifer there was nothing to get concerned about—"She wouldn't know what to do with herself without Dad." What a laugh. She had her next move all lined up.

"What do you think those buildings are for?" Teddy asked, bringing me around after the long, silent walk down the beach. We'd come farther than we had before, drawing even with the first of the two metal buildings.

"Let's go find out," I said. It was a relief to think about something else.

The windows all across the front of the building were painted white. Over the door was a sign that said *LABORATORIO SALAZAR.*

The door was locked and no one was around. We tried to find a spot in the windows where we could see in, but there wasn't one. We looked around the back and found plenty of windows and another door, but they were as curiosity-proof as the others.

Teddy wrinkled his nose. "Something's dead around here."

Now that he mentioned it, I caught a whiff myself. He was right. The sweet and pungent scent of decay was unmistakable. "Let's check it out," I said enthusiastically, on the spur of the moment. The death-smell must have addled my brain.

Teddy looked up at me dubiously. I was putting together the connection, the reason why locating the source made my kind of sense. Ah yes. Find something that stinks in the morning, find something that stinks in the afternoon.

"What, do you want to hide your head in the sand?" I asked theatrically. "Ignorance is bliss?"

He didn't know what prompted that display, but of course he'd seen me get weird before.

"It doesn't sound fun to me."

"C'mon, it won't kill you. Maybe you'll learn something."

I led him down a dirt track through the dense coconut

palms. If it hadn't been trashed out with so many old tires, bottles, cans, and so on, it would have been a beautiful grove. Soon we had to cup our noses and mouths with our hands, to try to filter the increasingly cloying and pungent stench. I had the source figured for some bloated cows—I'd seen that before—but I began to wonder as the smell grew worse than I could have imagined.

"Let's go back," I heard Teddy plead. "I don't care what it is."

"We gotta be close now."

We were. The track turned a corner and we could see ahead to a clearing with a huge mound in it covered with moving black spots.

A few more steps and we could tell the spots were large birds. As we neared, we saw they were tearing at some kind of meat. Then hundreds of them, buzzards and ravens, filled the air and stridently protested our intrusion.

"What is it?" Teddy said.

I couldn't tell. One end of the hill gleamed mostly white with bones, while the other showed plenty of flesh. The stench attacked us so overpoweringly I wasn't sure I could handle it.

"I'm going to throw up," Teddy said.

"Don't think about it. Hold your nose."

We walked closer, toward the whiter end of the hill, close enough for Teddy to recognize the shapes the bones took. "Oh, Travis," he cried, "—they're turtles!"

Then I could see the pattern. I was looking at a hill of sea turtle carcasses. "Casey didn't tell us anything about this," I said.

Teddy swooned and went down on one knee. I walked over to the bottom of the hill, looked around, and saw something truly bizarre—the bones of a human hand picked clean by the birds and bleached by the sun. I picked it up and yelled "Look at this!" and then went over and showed it to Teddy.

"That's a turtle's flipper," he said.

I was blown away, there was so little difference.

"I don't get it," I said. "What's going on here?"

I led Teddy a little farther around the hill, where the flies swarmed in the millions and a few brave ravens tore greedily at bits of rotting meat. Here the sun and the birds hadn't reduced the turtles to bones, and I could recognize them all too well, their beaks, their eye sockets, the leather around their necks and arms, the green plates on their shells, their flippers.

If you looked a little closer you could tell they'd all been butchered. I saw a raven ripping at a mass of intestines. I fired my beer bottle at him as hard as I could, but missed. He sprang away a little, looked at me with a cold eye, then went right back to it. I grabbed Teddy's pop bottle, fired, and missed again.

The air was thick with flies and their buzzing was unbelievably loud in my ears. I saw Teddy down on his knees throwing up. I grabbed him and yelled, "Let's get out of here!" and we ran down a road that looked like it would take us back to the beach. "I'm sorry, Teddy" I said as we ran, and I meant it. "I didn't have any idea."

The road angled off to the south. Up ahead we could see the second metal building. After a few minutes we could see that the road we were on led right up to a garage door in the back of the building. There were a few windows here and there, none painted. "I might as well check it out," I said.

Teddy slumped down on the ground and mumbled, "I'll wait here."

When I got back he asked wearily, "What was it?"

I took a good look at him. He couldn't take any more.

"A bunch of old ladies varnishing sea shells," I told him.

He didn't exactly look like he believed that, but he didn't object, either.

When we walked around the end of the building, a flatbed truck was backing up to a door there. The flatbed was stacked with dozens of live sea turtles writhing on their backs. Teddy looked at me like I'd betrayed him. I couldn't handle any of it any longer. "What'd you want me to tell you?" I yelled at him. "That this place is a concentration camp?"

 16 ≈

THE TURTLES were stacked about four deep. We could see them through the stakes around the side of the flatbed. Teddy reached through and touched one, we were that close. Underneath they were pretty well pinned, but the ones on top flailed their flippers and craned their necks trying to right themselves. Some men came out of the building, formed a "turtle brigade," and started passing them inside. The uncanny thing was, with the exception of a few flippers thudding against the stakes, the whole writhing mass of them made not a sound. I've heard pigs going to the slaughter—they yell bloody murder. These turtles were infinitely more polite. Only their eyes were screaming.

I could never take helplessness. When my grandfather was dying, he was on a respirator and couldn't talk.

He kept trying to write messages on paper, but they were totally unintelligible. Then he tried making letters with his finger one at a time in the air, but it was hopeless. I tried so hard to think of how he could communicate whatever it was he was so desperate to say, it was like I became him and it was me lying there on my back trapped without speech. It tore me up. After awhile he tried shaping a few simple words with his lips. Finally he got through to us. He was saying "I love you" over and over. I don't know if I could have managed like he did or not. Probably not.

When the last turtle had been taken inside, we walked out on the beach and had a look around. To the south, a pier jutted into the bay, and past it several long lines of poles ran up the beach. Both the pier and the pen, if that's what it was, were on a much larger scale than those on the north end of the Playa Tortugas.

Teddy spotted Casey climbing from his boat onto the pier. I told Teddy we should go see him. I thought he had some explaining to do.

Two motorboats were coming in off the bay toward us as we walked along the pier. Teddy froze when we got real close to Casey, who sat cross-legged and wrote on a clipboard. I nudged Teddy and whispered, "Go ahead, see what he has to say." Teddy tapped him on the back. Casey turned around and saw Teddy right there and me behind him. He started into that golden smile, but his face clouded over fast.

"We saw all those dead turtles back there," Teddy blubbered.

"The dump? Back in the trees?"

He glanced up at me and saw I was pretty burnt. "So you have," he said.

"How come you didn't tell us?" Teddy asked.

Casey knelt by Teddy and put a hand on his shoulder. "I was hoping you and Travis would've flown back home before you found out. Maybe I should have."

I watched the two boats pull in. Both of them were a good twenty feet long. Both were crammed full of sea turtles on their backs. "Here come the so-called fishing boats," I said.

The boats docked next to his. The men in the bows sprang out and tied them up. A man knee-deep in turtles reached into a cooler, tossed *refrescos* around, and the four of them kidded and joked in rapid-fire Spanish. I couldn't understand a word they said, but the feeling reminded me of the camaraderie that American loggers, longshoremen, and ironworkers share after a hard day's work filming beer commercials.

I heard the flatbed, then saw it backing toward the end of the pier. Teddy stood there staring down into the boats at the thrashing turtles. Then his face went glassy and he said absently, "Sailing ships used to keep them alive for months on long voyages."

"Time out for an historical footnote," I announced.

"On their backs—that's right," Casey said, ignoring my remark. "Sea turtles can't turn themselves over, so it was a convenient way to keep fresh meat. The turtles were in agony of course."

"How do you know?" I challenged. I felt like dishing it out. Before, I'd thought he was really something, but now I could see his feet were made of clay.

He studied me for a second, then said in a kindly sort of way, "They're just as full of nerves as you and me, Travis."

The men in the boats started to hand up the turtles.

75

"We'd better get out of their way," Casey said. As the truck reached the end of the pier, we jumped off its southern side. Somehow Teddy hadn't noticed the large, three-sided pole enclosure before. Now he asked Casey about it. Casey looked over there, and didn't seem too pleased.

"Looks like a turtle stockade to me," I said.

"That's what it is," he said wearily.

"Are there any turtles in there?" Teddy had to know.

The Mexicans started to load the truck, and Casey sprang back onto the pier. "Take a look," he said. "I have to count these turtles."

We walked up the beach past the high-tide mark and around the near side of the pen, then down to the water-line inside. We waded out and found them everywhere we looked. "There's hundreds in here!" Teddy yelled back to Casey.

"Their fate hasn't been decided yet," he called.

We waded around among the turtles until the truck drove back to the slaughterhouse, and then he joined us. Teddy asked, "What are these turtles doing in here?"

"They're females that laid their eggs during the last *arribada* a month ago. They were caught before they could make it back to the water."

"Aren't they protected?" Teddy objected. "They're endangered!"

"Nesting turtles always have been protected, but this fellow Domingo, who runs the show, talks a good line and has some influential friends. The Bureau of Fisheries granted a variance just for him. But we're still hoping we can save them. The Mexican conservationists have a restraining order to keep him from slaughtering these turtles in the pen until he can prove that his egg-hatching scheme works."

"Egg hatching?"

"Have you seen the other building?"

"*Laboratorio Salazar?*"

"Right—the one they keep locked up, with the painted windows. The eggs from the slaughtered females are being hatched in there. We hope."

"Wait a minute," I said. "How come you said *nesting* turtles have always been protected? If you can catch them offshore, what difference does it make?"

"Up until this year, there were quotas on the number they could take offshore. They were too high, but nothing like this year's—it's really no quota at all. That's why only a few turtles are getting through to the beach."

"So how many have you counted?"

He hesitated, and I thought he wouldn't say, but then he muttered, "Over fifty thousand."

I was shocked. I had no idea. But then, it sounded right—we'd seen the carcasses.

"An entire generation," Casey said.

"They're killing them all!" Teddy cried.

"That's what I've tried to get through to Domingo Salazar, many times."

"*Señor!*" we heard someone calling. We turned and saw a striking figure standing on the beach, a big man dressed for power in a dark, tailored suit. His graying hair and mustache complemented his bearing and lent him an air of dignity.

"Speak of the devil," Casey said under his breath.

"So this is the dirtball," I said under mine.

Casey waded slowly toward him, and we followed.

"*Buenos dias, señor,*" Domingo said expansively as they shook hands. "I want to make sure that you are invited to the Grand Opening of the laboratory tomorrow."

"Oh, I'll be there," Casey said quickly.

Domingo overlooked Casey's tone. "Good. Your fears will be pacified." Everything about his manner reflected self-confidence: it was obvious he was used to having his way, and he didn't regard Casey, in his muscle shirt and swimming trunks, as much of a threat.

To everyone's surprise, especially Domingo's, it was Teddy who took him on. "They don't all hatch at once," he said out of the blue. "What do you do with them after they hatch?"

Domingo took a good look at Teddy, with his white-blond hair, and glanced at me. It crossed my mind that he was wondering if we were Casey's kids.

"Who are these . . . ?"

"Their family is on vacation in Punta Blanca," Casey explained. "They're very interested in sea turtles."

Domingo turned on the charm. "Good, good. I like to hear that." Then he said to Teddy, "Perhaps you would like to come to the Grand Opening tomorrow as well. But to answer your question, we keep the hatchlings in sea water . . . for the time being."

No sooner were these last words out of Domingo's mouth than Teddy pounced on them. "How do you know they'll be able to find their way back after they grow up?"

Domingo looked confused, and Casey was enjoying how off-balance Teddy had put him. "Good question," Casey said. "It's thought that they imprint on the beach in between the time they hatch and the time they reach the water. Teddy here's asking, how do you know you aren't preventing them from being able to return here as adults?"

Domingo looked from Casey to Teddy, as if he wasn't used to being ganged up on. He started to explain rather slowly. You could see he was making it up as he went: "Those in the sea water are not so many . . . we had to save them for the Grand Opening . . . to show that our incubation process works. The great majority, of course, will be released on the beach as soon as they hatch."

He'd been able to finish in a flurry of self-confidence, but Casey quickly speared him again. "How long does it take to make them pen-happy?"

Domingo hadn't missed the sarcastic edge in Casey's voice. "Come tomorrow, *señor,*" he huffed, visibly offended. "All your fears will be pacified." With that, he turned abruptly and walked away.

Watching him go, Teddy shook his head and wondered aloud, "Why don't they just leave all the turtles alone?"

"Greed," I said.

"That's a big part of it," Casey said, "but most of the people involved, including Domingo, really believe that the turtles are as countless as the fish in the sea."

"That must be why they come under the Bureau of Fisheries," I cracked.

"That's right. But the conservationists down here know better. The Mexican press is becoming concerned too, and some well-meaning laws have been passed."

"Like what?" I asked suspiciously.

He wasn't at all sure about my tone, but he continued. "They have to use every part of the turtle, for example.

Those bones in the dump will be turned into fertilizer."

I don't know why, but I have a tendency to shoot the messenger who brings the bad news. I'd been needling Casey ever since we found out about the slaughterhouse. Now I thought I had my best opening yet. "You're saying it's all right what they're doing."

That got his goat. He shook his clipboard as he looked me in the eye and raised his voice: "You think I enjoy documenting the extinction of a species? How do you think that makes me feel? I'll tell you one thing, though— I hope Domingo's hatching scheme is a big success, because if it's not, the ridleys will be as scarce as the loggerheads!"

Teddy was distressed with me, and even more distressed by what Casey was saying. "What can we do?" he asked urgently, as if there were an answer.

"Ab-so-lutely nothing," I said bitterly.

"No, Travis, you're wrong," Casey said with a gentle smile. "When they're almost gone, it's going to stop. People are going to come through—you gotta believe that. Ours is the only voice these turtles have."

He put his hand on Teddy's shoulder, and said, "We'll nurse them back. Some day tens of thousands of turtles will return to this beach. They'll be so thick you won't be able to walk through 'em. I really believe that."

Apologizing to him never crossed my mind. On the way back to Punta Blanca I thought of a hundred other travesties I couldn't do a thing about, like weapons in space and chemical warfare in Afghanistan. Cynicism and self-righteousness have always coursed through my veins like addictive drugs.

17

TEDDY AND I caught the last bus into Punta Blanca, or we would have gotten back even later. Jennifer was waiting for us out on the sidewalk in front of the hotel. She was talking to Bill, who was on his motorbike, and she didn't see us among the people coming and going. "I'm just afraid we'd miss them and make things worse," she was saying.

"Make what worse?" I demanded, making a sudden appearance.

She looked relieved, but that didn't last long. "Mom's really mad," she said theatrically. "I told you you couldn't just take off like that."

What a joke. Jennifer thought that would scare me. I loved it that my mother was mad. As mad as she might be, she couldn't be half as angry as me. On the bus ride back I'd seen her over and over on the beach with that schmuck, and my anger had taken a form as exquisitely perfect as a rose. "She is, huh?" I said.

Actually I didn't like this guy hanging around, checking out our dirty laundry. He had his own dirty laundry to worry about—every time I'd seen him he was wearing the same grubby T-shirt with the leaping marlin. I didn't like his face, either. He looked like a real piece of slime.

"Why are you so late?" Jennifer insisted.

"Hey, we had a rough day at the office."

Bill started up his motorbike. "See you around," he said to her, and took off.

Now it was my turn to grill her. "What's the deal with him?"

"He just offered to help."

"We don't need no stinking help."

Teddy and I went straight to our room, and Jennifer went to hers. I figured it was up to my mother to make the next move. With both me and Mom on the warpath, Teddy sought refuge in bed with a nature book. He hadn't spoken a word since we left the scene of the turtle slaughter. I went out onto the balcony for a few minutes and parboiled my brains some more.

When I came back into the room I sat back on my bed and stared at the stuffed frog on the nightstand. That shook Teddy's concentration. He sneaked peeks at me as I out-glowered that baleful frog on the bongos. The thing did have an evil look, like something out of a "Twilight Zone" show. Something that would come alive at night, spread filth and disease, set fires, stab people with knives, and so on.

"Go ahead, make my day," I whispered savagely, and tore an arm off.

Teddy, the poor kid, was horrified. He'd seen me do it, and saw me holding that frog's limb up in the air like it meant something.

"It was us or him," I told Teddy. "He was planning to do things to us with a fork—during the night. Don't worry, we'll be all right now. I don't think he'll be able to do much with one arm."

Teddy could tell I hadn't flipped out, that I was only probing the limits of normal weirdness. He tried a little smile, but it got no farther than the corner of his mouth. He didn't think my routine was very funny.

There was a knock on the door—I could tell it was my mother, and so could Teddy. I had my back to the door, and he was facing it. He looked to me, I didn't respond. Then came a longer series of knocks. He started getting uncomfortable. The third time, he got up and opened the door.

There was a pause, and then she called my name quietly. I still had my back to her so I wouldn't have to look at her face. "You wanna see me?" I said.

"I just want to have dinner in as peaceful a fashion as possible. It's getting late."

She sure didn't sound like she was on the warpath. In fact, she sounded rattled.

"We had a misunderstanding about our schedules," she continued. "Just knock on the door when you're ready."

With forced cheerfulness, she asked Teddy, "How are you, darling?"

"Fine, Mom," he said, in a hollow voice.

"Good. We'll see you in a few minutes."

We took a cab to what had to be the fanciest place to eat in all of Punta Blanca—Margarita Manny's. We'd been seeing the billboards and brochures ever since we arrived. The guidebook said Margarita Manny's was the place to go for the finest in food and atmosphere, and you just might rub elbows with a movie star or two. Jennifer was surprised that Mom was taking us there, but after thinking it over, I wasn't. She thought she'd salve her conscience by spending a lot of money on us.

Margarita Manny's clings on four levels to a dramatic hillside above the sea. We entered at the highest level through arches covered with flowering bougainvilleas, and were greeted by a pleasant maitre d' who asked if we had a reservation.

"No, I'm afraid we don't. . . ." my mother answered. "We thought, since it was so late . . ."

"We are very busy this evening, as you can see, but if you'd care to wait . . ."

My mother turned to Jennifer and said, "Since we're already here, we should probably make the most of it."

"That will be fine," she told the maitre d', and he turned us over to a flunky who led us to a second-level balcony commanding a spectacular view of the crashing surf and the sunset.

I've heard it said, "You can't eat the scenery," and I certainly agree. I was starving and I'm sure Teddy was too. We'd neglected to eat any lunch and then spent the afternoon throwing up.

As we settled into our seats at a table right on the rim of the balcony, the beautiful people around us were oohing and aahing at the sunset. I'll have to admit it was a classic, the sun so huge and orange it looked like it was going nova just for the occasion. I've never heard such classic oohs and aahs in my life. I guess nobody can make them like the rich and famous.

My mother seized the occasion to try to emote some cheerfulness. "Look at that! Isn't this incredible? Have you ever seen anything like it?" Her oohs and aahs could keep up with the best of them. With that kind of talent and her looks, she sure wasn't going to have any difficulty fitting in.

"It's really nice, Mom," Jennifer agreed. I thought it was sick, how a fourteen-year-old had to coddle her mother.

I stared at the sun and tried to find out if it was really true that the setting sun couldn't burn your eyes. With the briefest glance my mother's way I said, "I thought the Fiesta was the only time we were going out 'fancy.' "

"We deserve it. I thought it would give us a lift."

A waiter dropped by and said he'd be back to take our order. A cocktail waitress showed up after a long while, then returned some time later with sodas for us and a margarita for my mother. I forgave the cocktail waitress for taking her time because she wore a low-cut blouse.

When it was about dark and they'd lit the lamps, the waiter came back and took our order.

"You like it here?" I asked my mother.

There must have been something about my tone. "Travis . . ." my sister warned.

"Yes, it's beautiful," my mother replied.

I wrinkled my nose as if picking up a scent. "It smells funny to me."

"It doesn't smell funny," Jennifer insisted.

"Kinda like pigs," I said, still sniffing around. "Rich pigs."

No response. They thought if they ignored me I might cut it out.

But I was just getting warmed up. I tried my nose again and found the scent more favorable. "Hey, they smell pretty good. This isn't half-bad, rubbing elbows with 'em. Just think—they probably migrate down here every year, maybe twice a year. Maybe I'd like to be a rich pig too."

Jennifer was outraged. "Stifle it, Travis!"

But my mother, hanging onto her margarita and trying to sip from it, seemed to be suspended in a curiously powerless limbo.

A seasoned infighter like me knows when he's scored, and tries to open up the wound. You don't give your opponent time to recoup. "No kidding—I'm serious, I might really like it. How 'bout you, Mom?"

I guess the cat had her tongue. She couldn't say anything at all. She just stared off into space and tried to sip her margarita. I was able to look at her for once. There was a tic in her cheek.

Jennifer looked incredulously back and forth between me and my mother. Whatever nerve I'd hit, she'd never seen the like of it before. Teddy, of course, was trying to become invisible. The cocktail waitress came to my side and asked if we would care for another round. I don't know why she mistook me for the man of the family. "Yes please," my mother said.

The cocktail waitress had broken my concentration. Rhythm is so important when you're having a fight like this one. I eased off, brooded in my corner, and paced myself for the next round.

It seemed like hours were passing. It could have been minutes, I don't know. I remember my mother asking no one in particular, "How long ago did we order?"

Eventually the cocktail waitress returned with our drinks. This time she brought chips and salsa as well, on the house. "It feels better to get something into your stomach, anyway," my mother said. She'd recouped, at least on the surface. I couldn't have that. She asked, "What did you guys see today?"

She said it wearily, with a veneer of cheerfulness. I think she expected Teddy to answer. I saw him squirm and could tell he was picturing that stinking hill of turtle carcasses.

"Nothing out of the ordinary," I said blandly. And with sudden ferocity I followed that up with, "*Nothing to write home about.*"

Another hit. She was staggered.

"Why are you doing this, Travis?" I heard Jennifer plead, in tones of anguish.

Like a movie star with nerves of steel, I dipped another chip and ate it while I waited out the timing for my next line. Then I said to Jennifer, "Hey, I miss him. Don't you miss him?"

I snuck a glance at my mother. I used to love her, I suppose. But if she could stop loving my father, I could stop loving her. Sensing she didn't have the strength even to lift an arm, I administered the *coup de grâce* as I finally looked her full in the face. "How 'bout you, Mom? Don't you miss him?"

That did it. She broke. She burst out crying with

the volume all the way up. People from all over were checking us out, and my body temperature shot up about twenty degrees. Jennifer stared at me wildly, trying to find out if looks could kill, and I heard Teddy whimpering.

With her napkin in her face, my mother reached for her purse, threw a bundle of pesos on the table, and fled. Jennifer and Teddy followed right behind her, and I was left there holding the bag with all the rich and famous watching. I hope I didn't spoil their evening.

As I was making my exit, the waiter brought out our dinners. Great. Just great. I didn't even have the presence of mind to ask for a doggie bag.

They were waiting for me inside a cab. All of them were in the back seat. My mother was on the far side. She had her head in her hands and she was crying uncontrollably. Teddy was scared to death, and Jennifer gave me the evil eye.

The curb man for Manny's didn't let on like anything was wrong. *"Buenas noches,"* he told me pleasantly.

"Buenas snowshoes," I said. It seemed like the thing to say at the time.

 **18** ≈

WE TRUDGED PAST the Sol Mar's desk in various attitudes of defeat. It was going to be a long, hungry night.

"We have a call for you from your husband," the young woman behind the desk called.

My mother was terribly confused, like she was punch-drunk. She looked around to see who it was the clerk was talking to. There wasn't anybody else. "My husband?" she asked.

"He's been holding for thirty minutes—we can't use our telephone." She was still working on her nails, and she hadn't gotten any sweeter.

My mother dug in her purse for a fresh tissue. "You get on first," she told Jennifer.

Jennifer's end of the conversation sounded like this:

"Hi, Dad.

"Just fine.

"It's really pretty down here. Lots of beautiful beaches. It's warm, too.

"I miss you, Daddy. I love you. Here's Teddy."

Here's what Teddy had to say:

"Travis and I saw some sea turtles, Dad! Ridleys!

"We even got to swim around with them in the ocean—we met a marine biologist.

"I love you too, Dad. Travis is right here."

Teddy signaled me over. I didn't exactly want to talk with my father. I'd thought about getting on the elevator as soon as I heard he was on the phone, but I stuck around to hear what my mother would say. At the moment, she was sitting in an armchair and drumming her fingers, with her back to us.

"Hello, Travis, how are you?"

I can't stand character tests. I feel like a bug with a pin through its back and its legs still moving. All I want to do is get free. "Just great," I answered enthusiastically.

It was really eerie hearing his voice. It was like I knew him from another lifetime, when I was very young. I couldn't even have described at that moment what he looked like.

"Teddy told me you swam with some sea turtles."

"Yeah, it was great."

"I should have been there, Travis."

He didn't sound conversational at all—his voice was too loaded with emotion.

"You would have really liked it," I said.

"Right—I mean I should have come to Mexico with you. I guess I was on a martyr trip."

He wanted to be real, and all I wanted was to get off the phone. I couldn't tell what he knew, and I didn't want to find out. When I didn't comment at all, he asked, "How's your mother?"

"Fine," I said.

"Would you put her on?"

Then he added quickly, "I love you, Travis." That was the second time he'd said it. The first was back at the airport, to everybody. I always knew he loved me, but I never heard him say it before, not like that. It's embarrassing enough to hear a private man bare his soul, especially when he's your father. In this context it only reinforced my impression that the sky was falling. I pretended I'd already left the phone.

My mother had pulled herself together somewhat. I handed the phone to her and took her place over in the armchair.

"Hello, Dan," she said tentatively.

For a long time Dad was talking and she didn't say anything. Then she said, "I'm glad you didn't. We'll be home the day after tomorrow."

Didn't what? Had he been thinking about joining us?

Next time she said, "Don't go into that, please."

Another long pause, then, "Yes, there's a one percent chance, maybe two percent. I don't know anything right now."

I knew what the numbers meant. There was a one to two percent chance she wouldn't get a divorce. That was news.

Her next offering: "Quit apologizing."

Then, "Well, see you soon."

And, "Good-bye."

≈19

THEY WENT UPSTAIRS to our rooms. I stayed behind in the lobby and they didn't object.

In a few minutes Jennifer was back, hopping mad. I can almost picture her now, hopping out of the elevator and across the lobby. She came on like gangbusters: "How could you be so cruel?"

"Calm down, Jennifer. I told him we were doing fine, same as you did."

"You know what I'm talking about—what you did to Mom."

"Calm down!"

"Don't tell me to calm down! Tell me, why did you do that?"

Obviously, she thought the answer was "unadulterated meanness." She had no idea it had more to do with "adulterated" meanness. I took the measure of her innocence, and answered, "That's for me to know."

Believe it or not, I'd planned all day to shelter her from the truth, same as Teddy.

"What do you mean by that?"

Her third-degree interrogation was beginning to erode my resolve. I wanted to vindicate myself. "Tell me this," I said melodramatically, "—why didn't she fight back?"

"She was too hurt."

"Hurt and what else?"

"You tell me."

It's no fun to swallow rat poison, even if by accident, and not pass it around. I decided I'd give her an introductory dose. "I'm not going to tell you. You watch her and see for yourself."

"What are you talking about?"

"Tell me, why hasn't she gone on any of those tours you wanted to take, like a boat trip?"

"She wanted to this afternoon, but you'd already split."

"Yeah? How about tomorrow? That's our last full day. Has she said anything about tomorrow?"

"No . . ."

The blood was pumping in my temples. I raised my voice: "I'll tell you why . . ."

"Why?"

"I think she has other plans."

Now I really had her upset. "Like what? How do you know?"

"Just watch her tomorrow, and see if she doesn't disappear again."

"Like you've been doing?"

"Yeah—like that. Then start asking yourself a few questions. And don't you try to sway her."

I thrashed furiously in my sleep that night. I couldn't begin to process it all. I can't remember what I dreamed, and I'm glad of it. Something truly awful woke me up in the middle of the night. I lay there sweating, conscious of every little sound in the street. That one-armed frog was staring me in the face. There was no chance I'd get back to sleep.

Involuntarily I started going over the awful things that had happened the day before. It was all too vivid. I don't know what was worse, the twisted shapes of my dreams, or this total realism of waking memory.

"Travis, are you awake?" Teddy whispered.

"Yeah."

"I can't get back to sleep."

"Me neither."

I got up and went to the sliding glass door, and looked out on the little urban farm. A rooster shook his wings out and cut loose with a clarion call. He wanted to be the first in all of Mexico to announce the new day. What with the full moon and the street lights, it's no wonder his clock was haywire.

"Want to take a walk?" I asked. "We'd be back before they got up."

He looked relieved. "Sure."

We walked out of the south end of town and up the winding road toward the Playa Tortugas. When we reached the top, we scrambled out to a huge, flat-topped boulder on the very edge of the cliff. The full moon rode over the sea and lit every swell and wave from the horizon to the exploding surf below.

For a long time neither of us spoke. Teddy might have been content to sit there indefinitely and air out his soul in that white light, but after awhile it got to me. If you don't have your head in a good place, beauty like that can be excruciating. I couldn't take it any longer and broke the spell with words: "A peaceful place, or so it looks from space."

Teddy smiled. The words are from a Grateful Dead song my father likes to sing.

Teddy pointed down to the south. "You can see the laboratory from here. Do you think we can go to the Grand Opening?"

"It's our last day—we'll just have to wait and play it by ear."

"I hope so."

It seemed like he wanted to say something more. "What is it?" I asked.

"I had a dream I was swimming with thousands of turtles far out at sea."

"Tell me about it."

"It wasn't like I was *like* one of them—I *was* one of them. I could feel my flippers and everything. I didn't even have to come up and breathe hardly. There were turtles all around me, and we were swimming together on a long journey. It was what flying must feel like for birds, only the air was water."

Turtles as birds! That's what I'd been thinking when we snorkeled with them. The way he talked, he made that feeling wash over me again and my eyes filled with tears. "That's really great," I mumbled.

He had that faraway look on his face, yet at the same time he was talking to me. "No one knows how they navigate over thousands of miles, always back to the same beach. There's a theory that they navigate by the stars. The funny thing about my dream, Travis—*I* was navigating by the stars. We were all doing it together."

He paused, and then he added, "Some day maybe I can find out if that theory's true."

"Sounds like you already have," I said.

20

As STARVED as I was, I was almost afraid to go to breakfast in the morning. To my relief, no mention was made of the disaster at Margarita Manny's. My mother seemed willing to "forgive and forget."

Teddy asked if he and I couldn't go to the hatchery's Grand Opening that afternoon. To my complete surprise my mother suggested we all go, that she'd like to find out what it was all about. Teddy was delighted and Jennifer couldn't have been more pleased. She shot me a smug "You were saying? . . ."

But then my mother suggested we spend the morning at the beach on the Strip, and it was my turn to give Jennifer a little nonverbal "I told you so."

Once we arrived at the Strip, I took off after reminding Jennifer that she wasn't supposed to stick to Mom like

97

glue. If I'd wanted to prevent her from meeting this guy Mitch, I could have done that myself. I wanted to give my mother every chance to betray us. Why? How am I supposed to know? I'm not a psychiatrist.

Time was running out for meeting someone. This was my last chance to savor the beach scene at Punta Blanca, maybe meet somebody and make something happen. A good number of the sunbathers were brand-new arrivals, perfectly white. I decided that the best feature of a major destination resort is the daily *arribada* of beautiful women. The supply is inexhaustible. In front of the Oceano Hacienda I found a raven-haired beauty lying on her stomach—you guessed it—with her top unhooked. You already know how I sneak in on the blind side, spread out my beach towel, and so on. That's what I did. She never even heard me glide in there.

After awhile of course, she got cramped with her head to that one side, and turned it my way. By that time I had my eyes closed and was probably snoring lightly for effect. It was my intention to strike up a conversation somehow when I woke up.

When I did look, she was up on her elbows a bit and holding her top up against her, looking right at me too. "It's you again," she said.

Oh, no. She was the same one who'd drop-kicked me down the beach before. Thirtyish and unabashed. How was I supposed to know it was her? She was wearing a different bikini.

One thing I should have noticed though, she hadn't just gotten off the plane. There was no sign of a strap-line across her back, and she had the skin color of a

Mexican Indian. Her tan and her jet-black hair made a deadly combination.

She looked right through me and said, "What is it with you, anyway?"

"What do you mean?"

"Remember?—a few days ago?—we went through this same routine?"

The way she said it, I glimpsed a bit of humor, like at least she was getting off on how ludicrous the situation was. Then she practically smiled, and said, "What kind of strange bird are you, anyway?"

Good question. I thought I might as well try to answer it.

"Bird?" I repeated thoughtfully. "What kind of bird? Vulture, I guess."

"Hardly an endangered species," she said with a grin. She reached back and hooked her top, then sat up and said, "So how do you like Punta?"

I couldn't believe she was going to talk to me. "Oh great," I said. "I really love it."

"Come over and tell me about your vacation."

I sat down beside her thinking furiously about what I should say. She had the most lovely hazel eyes. At first I thought I would tell her I was down there by myself, but just as quickly I knew she wouldn't believe it. Instead I told her I was with my mother and sister and little brother, and how my Dad couldn't get away from work.

"That's too bad," she said.

"It's no big deal," I said. There's no way I wanted to get into all that. Without really thinking about it I steered the conversation toward Teddy—he's so easy to talk about. I found myself telling her how much he knew about natural science, how he was crazy about turtles, what a great kid he was. Really it was more like a monologue. As long as I had her attention I just kept going. It was obvious she was alone and didn't mind having somebody to talk to.

"You really love your little brother," she said after awhile.

"I guess so."

"That's nice. I never had any brothers or sisters."

I went on and told her about how we swam with the turtles. I tried to describe how beautiful it was and how great I felt because I could tell she was getting off on it. Really animated, I proceeded to tell her how Teddy had actually seen one lay its eggs and how the two of us had come across hatchlings going for the sea. Next thing I knew I had adopted an urgent tone and was telling her about the guy picking up the hatchlings. I was within an eyelash of getting into the hill of carcasses and the slaughterhouse when I realized what a turn-off that would be and stopped dead in my tracks.

It was pretty awkward how I'd left my story hanging. All concerned, she asked, "What was he doing?"

I recovered fast. "I think they raise some for zoos."

She went for it. "I saw some at Sea World once."

"How much longer are you going to be here?" I asked quickly.

She reached for her sunscreen. I could tell she was thinking about me. "I think I've had about enough sun," she said. She hesitated as she was about to squeeze some into her hand. "I'm leaving tomorrow."

"Can I help with that—maybe get your back?"

She balked for a second, then said "Sure."

With my heart going wild, I took the lotion and she turned around, and I went to work on her back.

Now was my chance, I knew, to try to get something going if I hadn't blown it already. "Tell me about yourself," I said.

"Oh, there's not much to tell . . ."

"You came down by yourself?"

She heaved a sigh, almost wasn't going to answer, and then said with a grim smile, "Recovering from a divorce."

Saying the words almost made her cry. I'm glad she was facing away so I didn't have to look at her just then.

"I'm sorry," I said, but really I wasn't sorry at all. My heart beat even harder. Actually I thought it was great. If she was married she'd be with somebody and none of this would be happening.

"I'm going to have to be going," she said with a sigh. "I have a windsurfing lesson."

Now I'd done it. But maybe there was still a chance. . . . "Since you're leaving tomorrow, I wonder if I could see you later?"

"Later?"

"This evening, maybe?—I really like talking with you."

She turned around, and I set the sunscreen down slowly. "I've enjoyed talking with you too," she said. For a few long seconds she didn't say anything, and then she added, "You don't have to be with your family?"

"'Heck no, I'm with them all the time. I could come over after dinner—which hotel are you in?"

I held my breath as those words hung a long time

in the air. What was she thinking? I think she was really lonely and liked me both.

"I'll be packing . . . you could tell me some more about your little brother and the sea turtles."

"Sure."

"I'm in 837 in the Oceano Hacienda."

21

COULDN'T BELIEVE IT! Sometimes you get lucky! Room 837, in the Oceano Hacienda. Today, tonight, tonight's the night. Already I felt radiant, at peace for once with myself. It was comforting to discover I wasn't as deranged as I'd thought. All I needed was a little love. After tonight I could work on becoming a decent human being.

My mother was with Teddy and Jennifer when I got back. Jennifer and Mom had buried Teddy in sand and were trying to build a castle on his stomach. "Be still," Jennifer told him. "Quit breathing so hard." Teddy was giggling. They were so cheerful they were giddy.

"You guys all been here hanging out?" I asked Jennifer.

"We've been right here," she said with a big grin.

"Are we all still going to the lab opening?"

"That's the plan."

My mother suggested we stop at the big open market on the way back to the hotel. "The book says we shouldn't miss it."

"Sure," I said.

"Your allowances must have run out. Maybe you'll find some souvenirs at the market."

Teddy was big-eyed. So was I. She handed each of us three thousand pesos. That's big bucks—about twenty dollars. She kissed me on the cheek and said, "Take that, tough guy. Don't spend it all in one place."

"Mucho dinero," I whistled. "Good deal—thanks."

During the cab ride to the market I decided that the universe was unfolding as it should. She'd told Mitch she wasn't sure about his little car trip, and then she told Dad there was a two percent chance. I'd overheard her say she loved me, too—I was ready to think about that now. I decided I could forgive her having an affair if she'd stay with Dad. Lots of the married couples who go through this manage to put it back together because they love each other. They find out that's what counts more than anything else. I was sure my mother still loved my father. Maybe she'd realize that all the things she wanted but couldn't have weren't very important anyway.

As we got out of the cab, Jennifer told my mother that she hadn't found anything for herself yet, that she should pick out an embroidered dress or blouse and buy it.

"Maybe you gave us too much money," I suggested.

"Don't worry about me—I just haven't found anything I liked."

Apparently she was on a martyr trip too. That was a new one on me. She'd never been reluctant to spend money on herself that I could remember.

"Maybe you'll find something here," Jennifer said.

We arranged to meet in half an hour, and Teddy and I took off.

The market covered maybe a square block, yet we realized within a few steps that we'd have to stick close or we'd lose each other for sure. The place was a labyrinth teeming with sound, color, smells, and bustling activity. We happened to start out in the fruit, rows upon winding rows of ripe, riper, and rotting fruit. Large, dark women in little stalls crowded with crates of papayas and pineapples cried out to us as we passed, hawking their wares or maybe teasing us, I couldn't tell. One of them snatched at Teddy's white-blond hair, and then they giggled. We were jostled by shoppers ripe like the fruit, and skinny mongrel dogs ran between our feet. A woman in the tomatoes was milking her goat. A girl no older than Jennifer nursed a baby. Around a few corners the aisle was blocked by a boy unloading bananas. We stopped and looked around, and four large, fleshy women were suddenly trying to sell us some. We looked to each other, which must have meant something, because two had bananas peeled as quick as you please and were urging us to sample them. They were tasty.

I started negotiating with the two women for a bunch of bananas. That was a mistake.

I'm too tough a haggler, I guess. One of the women

clammed up and the other wagged her forefinger at me, then indicated she'd sell me a blackened bunch off the ground for the price I'd offered. The women looking on started to get on my case. Something or other made me think they were making obscene wisecracks at my expense. I checked to see if my fly was open.

I thought I'd better get out of there, so I quickly reached a compromise price on the bananas, then pulled out the bills Mom had given me. That was another mistake. Now they really thought I was a cheeseball. I could have bought three truckloads with that. Teddy had some change and bailed me out. We beat a hasty retreat with our ten-cent bunch of bananas.

After Bananaland we cruised through the vegetables, where I learned what has to be the choicest word in the entire Spanish language. It's *cacahuates*, and it means "peanuts." Say it slowly and accent the third syllable, which is pronounced "wah" as in "wah-wah pedal," and you'll see what I mean. *Ca-ca-hua-tes*. It's far more evocative than "peanuts" or "goobers," I'm sure you'll agree. We bought two handfuls and headed into the buzzing fury of the meat section. Just to be gross I reminded Teddy that thousands of those flies were successfully laying eggs in the meat. He said that didn't bother him a bit, but did I know that there are monstrous-looking insects that live at the base of each of my eyelashes?

Around the corner from the seafood, we came across a stall with a boy and a man selling live iguanas. Teddy flipped out. On their twine leashes, the iguanas resembled miniature green dinosaurs. One of them must have been five feet long from its spine-crested head to the

106

tip of its tail. Teddy held it and admired it awhile, and the vendors didn't mind at all. They were hoping he'd buy it for dinner.

I knew iguanas weren't endangered, and suggested we buy the huge one, take him home for a pet, and save him from somebody else. Teddy said he might like to, but they would take it away from us at the border and quarantine it for months. It seems that American officials are paranoid that some exotic insect might try to sneak through customs hitching a ride on a lizard. And come to find out, human eyelash bugs have been sneaking through for years.

We discovered there was a whole covered section to the market in the back. There must have been over a hundred shops stuffed in there, crammed with more arts and crafts than you could shake sticks at. But we'd already seen our fill of straw hats, onyx bookends, and *huarache* sandals. Our prize discovery was a little shop full of smooth and highly polished carvings of animals in a lustrous, reddish-brown, and close-grained wood I'd never seen before.

The proprietor, a low-key guy with fluent English, told us they were made by the Seri Indians. We marveled at the workmanship. Every carving in the shop was a masterpiece as far as we were concerned. Our favorites were the marlins and the gulls, a great white shark, and an elephant. Until I found the sea turtle, that is.

I knew it was meant to be the moment I saw it: languishing among lions on a shelf by the floor, a single sea turtle. I held my breath, picked it up, and floated it across the room to Teddy. I guess he liked it. He looked like the archeologist who discovered King Tut's treasures must have looked, at the moment he first saw the boy-king's death mask gleaming with lapis lazuli and solid gold.

The carving was about ten inches long, smooth and heavy and symmetrical. The turtle was in the act of swimming, with its large front flippers extended like wings. The man whipped out a handkerchief and lovingly dusted it off for us. "Ironwood," he said. "Very fine for carving." Each of us held it and stroked its back, petted it on the top of the head, and admired its unlikely weight in our hands. On the underside of the shell it had a price tag—three thousand pesos.

"What do you think?" I asked Teddy.

He agonized over it, then finally shook his head. The price really had him intimidated. It was everything Mom had given him, and I'm sure he'd never spent that much at one shot in his life. "No thank you," he told the shopkeeper bashfully.

"Good," I said quickly, and pulled my own wad from my pocket. "Then I can get it for you. I just happen to have three thousand right here."

I handed it straight over to the guy, no haggling or anything. Maybe I could have gotten it for less, but that didn't seem important. I knew the price didn't begin to reflect its true value.

"*Gracias,*" the shopkeeper said.

"*Muchas gracias* yourself," I said, and handed the turtle over to Teddy.

As we left the shop, Teddy was protesting, "Travis, you shouldn't—"

"Shut your face. I want you to have it."

The kid was levitating. I felt pretty good myself.

22

AFTER WE BOUGHT the turtle we got some terrible directions to the restroom from a shoeshine boy, and we really got turned around in the service alleys behind the shops. At one point we came across a group of men sitting around a card table and I paused, thinking about asking them for help.

They didn't seem likely to be English speakers, I could see that. There was one old man with his mouth caved in; the rest were middle-aged. They looked poor. Only one had shaved in the last few days.

As we stood there we watched one take eggs from a cardboard box and break them into a pitcher. They were round like ping-pong balls, and they weren't brittle. The shell was more leathery, like a skin. Turtle eggs! This is what Casey was talking about. These guys think that the eggs make them more manly. And the table was set up in the back of the market because they were breaking the law.

When the pitcher was about half full, one of them added some red stuff I took for chili powder, and whipped the eggs with a fork. The old man produced Styrofoam cups, and five concoctions were poured.

As they chugged their "drinks," Teddy sidled up close enough to the table to see into the box, then came back to me with that urgency all over his face.

"There's probably thirty in there—maybe I can buy them!"

He jammed his fist into his pocket and came out with his roll of pesos.

"What for?"

"I could bury them back on the beach when nobody's looking."

What would this kid come up with next?

"What makes you think they're still good?"

"They wouldn't be eating them if they were spoiled—they were probably just dug up!"

He had to have those eggs. At first I was going to tell him to forget it, but then I got to thinking maybe he was right and they would hatch. So I pocketed his pesos and approached the men, who had finished drinking the eggs and were joking around. Even though I was standing right in front of them, they didn't seem to notice me until I cleared my throat. Then they broke off with each other and stared at me.

Most of them still had yellow slime caught in the stubble around their mouths. "*Tienen huevos?*" I asked tentatively. ("Do you have eggs?")

They looked to each other, and back to me, and didn't say anything. Things were getting strange.

"*Tienen huevos?*" I repeated, as friendly as I could.

One of them pointed at me while he looked at the others, and his face broke out in a toothy smile. They all cracked up, practically fell off their chairs slapping each other on the back and laughing at me.

Did I say something funny?

When their laughter subsided, one of them said to me very gravely, "*Sí, sí—y usted?*" ("Yes, yes—and you?")

My Spanish teacher had always said to ask "Are there any eggs?" not "Do you have any eggs?" but she never explained why. Now I knew.

They'd never seen the like of the two of us, I'm sure of that. In the course of negotiations they said something to the effect that these weren't "ordinary chicken eggs," and I said something to the effect that I knew they were from "the chicken of the sea," and therefore "more valuable than the terrestrial variety." They liked that. I think that's when they decided I was no sting operation, only a horny goofball.

I managed to buy the eggs, but even with some hard bargaining it cost Teddy everything he had. That was fine with him. He understood the law of supply and demand, and he knew ridley eggs were as scarce as hen's teeth.

When we came within sight of Jennifer and my mother waiting for us at the curb, Teddy ran over to them and showed them his ironwood sea turtle. I could hear him shouting, "Mom, look what Travis got me! Look what Travis got me!"

She had it in her hands, was feeling its polished perfection as I walked up. "It's absolutely beautiful, Teddy." She turned it over and saw the price tag, and looked at me, well, lovingly.

"Some tough guy," she repeated, and gave me another peck on the cheek. The one I got earlier was practically unprecedented, so what in the world was going on?

"Look what Paco here blew his wad on!" I said as I opened the top of the box on my hip.

Jennifer and my mother cautiously peered inside. They were totally nonplussed.

"Garden variety turtle eggs!" I announced.

"They were poached," Teddy said quickly, as if that explained everything. "I'm going to bury them back in the sand at the Playa Tortugas this afternoon."

My mother looked pretty chagrined—after all, Teddy had just blown twenty-some dollars on turtle eggs. Under the conditions, she showed considerable restraint. "Don't you think you're taking your—interest—a little too far, dear?"

"Not if they hatch!"

"We'll never know," I pointed out.

My mother said cheerfully, "Well, I suppose it's the thought that counts."

23

IN THE CAB on the way back to the Sol Mar,
Jennifer showed us her own treasure, an embroidered
muslin blouse featuring a large parrot among huge tropical flowers. There must have been a million stitches in
it. She said Mom had found a beautiful embroidered
dress that looked wonderful on her and didn't buy it,
but she should have.

"I just had to get outside," my mother said. "I was
starting to feel light-headed. As a matter-of-fact, I don't
feel so good right now."

Jennifer always feels bad herself when other people
are sick. "What's the matter, Mom?"

"I don't know—I think it's both my head and my
stomach. I better lie down when we get back to the
hotel."

"We've been so lucky up till now," Jennifer said.

"I know. I hope it's not '*Turista*.' "

I can't say I felt bad for her. The wheels were turning and I was getting suspicious.

Teddy was worried. "Can we still go to the Grand Opening?"

"Yes, darling, I'm just not sure I'll be able to. We'll see after I lie down for a few minutes."

I had worries of my own. I was starting to worry about my rendezvous at the Oceano Hacienda. She was so self-assured, and I wasn't at all.

After we got back to the hotel and my mother had "rested" awhile, she said for us to go ahead without her. "I'm just not strong enough."

"I'll stay with you," Jennifer said.

"No, you don't have to do that."

"I want to."

"Jennifer, I'll be fine. If I feel up to it, I might even go back to the market and buy that dress. I don't know what I'll do—I'll probably just stay here."

Jennifer glanced at me, asking in effect, "Is this what you were talking about?"

I shrugged a "yes."

Jennifer was hamstrung. She couldn't say, "Hold everything—would somebody tell me what's going on here?" because she knew I wouldn't tell her, and she couldn't exactly ask Mom. Mom had always confided in her. They trusted each other.

"You really don't want me to stay with you?" was all she could manage.

My mother looked relieved that Jennifer had given up. "I'll be better after a good rest, don't worry about me. Run along and have a good time."

There was a hollow feel to her voice: indecisive, lonely, distant. She was right there with us, and she'd never been farther away. I didn't say a word, even though I could tell she wasn't that sold on running off on us. I could have stopped her but I didn't feel like it.

My anxieties about the evening were getting out of control. I wished there was something like a wonder drug I could take. Then I thought about Teddy's turtle eggs. It sounds stupid, I know, but I needed a little insurance. Even if it didn't do anything, it would give me a psychological edge, a "placebo effect."

So I stole one, and hid it for later.

24

WHEN WE WERE halfway down the Playa
Tortugas and Teddy was content that no one was in
sight, he selected a spot above the high-tide mark and
began to dig furiously, like a dog going after a gopher.
Jennifer and I were posted to keep watch. This was
serious business.

As for me, I was relieved to have something going
on for the afternoon. For a time I could get my mind
out of Room 837. The anticipation was burning me
up.

Jennifer really enjoyed herself watching Teddy dig
that hole. "I finally got here," she said wistfully. "You
guys assume I wouldn't be interested, but I am."

"Ca-ca-hua-tes," I replied.

"What's that?"

"Peanuts." I pulled a plastic pack from my back pocket. "Want some?"

Teddy placed the eggs in a clutch in the hole he'd dug. He stood back and inspected his work. "Maybe they're too deep. They can't be too deep or too shallow."

One at a time, he carefully returned them to the box, then filled in the hole a little.

Jennifer and I ate peanuts and kept on the lookout for spies. Jennifer tried again to get me to talk. This time she came right to the point. "What's going on with Mom, Travis?"

That's all it took to get the juices flowing. "Hey, hear no evil, see no evil, speak no evil—that's my policy. I don't know nothin' about nothin'."

She turned away and helped Teddy plant the eggs, then cover them with sand. Afterwards they made everything look natural.

Teddy inspected the area from every angle. Something wasn't right. He took off his thongs and walked barefoot right over the spot. Then he was satisfied. "Good job, Paco," I told him.

As we walked away he glanced over his shoulder, as if those baby turtles might be surfacing already. "I really think they're going to hatch."

I remember once when Teddy was a toddler I found him sticking duck feathers in the flowerbed. When I asked him what he was doing, he said he was going to grow some ducks. Compared to those ducks, these turtles were going to be a lead-pipe cinch.

Teddy hurried us down the beach, afraid he'd miss the Grand Opening. As it turned out we walked right in the open door of the lab and joined the show. I doubt we were all that late, and in any case we didn't miss anything. It didn't look like any Grand Opening I'd ever seen. No hot dogs, soda, nothing. Domingo was standing in front of the first of six long rows of metal bins filled with sand. He was orating magnificently to about thirty people, all men. I can't speak for the others but the vocabulary Domingo used sure had me bamboozled. I couldn't understand a thing he said, but it sure sounded good.

With his height and blond hair, Casey stood out. Even though he wore a short-sleeved shirt and slacks, he'd underdressed—all the Mexicans wore suits. Nonetheless he looked impressive. Maybe it was his forearms.

Teddy led us to him and caught his eye. Casey acknowledged Jennifer and flashed us each a warm smile. Teddy whispered, "What's he saying?" Casey was listening hard and signaled him to wait. I nodded toward Domingo and asked Jennifer, "Would you buy a used car from this guy?"

"It sure is warm in here. Do you know what he's saying?"

"He's extolling the virtues of pre-chewed *cacahuates.*"

Domingo ended a long stretch of monologue with a grand gesture. Evidently he'd made a joke because some of the group were laughing. Some of the others however, including Casey, were shaking their heads.

Casey gave us a quick summary. "He said that close to one hundred percent of the eggs laid on the beach used to be dug up by poachers, but now they've solved the problem by removing the eggs from the slaughtered females and incubating them here in the laboratory."

I asked what the joke was. Casey whispered to me,

so Teddy wouldn't hear, "He said they remove them by cesarian section."

Even I didn't think that was funny. I couldn't work up much appreciation for Domingo. After seeing his slaughterhouse, I thought he was a real Nazi. He should have been a PR man to that doctor at Auschwitz who conducted all those experiments on little kids and afterwards lined the shelves of his office with pickle jars full of their eyeballs. Domingo could have conducted tours for the VIPs who came to visit, and told jokes to make them feel at home.

Domingo pointed to the fluorescent lights suspended over the bins. I gathered he was explaining how they do a better job than the sun at hatching turtles. Then he had everybody follow him down the aisle a ways, and he stopped at one of the bins to create a photo opportunity for the press. Expounding all the while, he took off his suit jacket and dug in the sand until he uncovered some eggs, then covered them up again. I didn't get the point.

After that he led us over to three waist-high metal tanks against the wall, which each turned out to have about a hundred hatchlings swimming around and around in about a foot of water. From the look on the proud father's face, you knew this was the climax of the tour. He didn't hold anything back, and must have set some kind of a record for eloquence. Just when you thought he'd reached the absolute heights, he climbed for more.

Ten minutes later I was losing my mind with boredom. If I had a shotgun I could have blasted Domingo and put him out of his ecstasy. Actually that wouldn't have been a bad idea. Nothing else would have turned out the same if I'd done that. I would have gone to jail of course, but there are fringe benefits, like all the Mexican food you can eat.

Instead I started looking around checking everybody out. I watched the reactions on the audience's perspiring faces as they stood around in their tight black shoes. Most of them hung on Domingo's every word. I took them for officials or relatives or both. The conservationists Casey mentioned were easy to identify. They were frowning and they wore two-piece suits, as opposed to the three-piece suits of the vested interests. Also they foamed slightly at the mouth. It's good to know that Mexico too has its "rabid environmentalists."

Finally Domingo finished with a flourish, his partisans applauded, and Casey translated the water-tank speech. "He says these are eighty percent of the trial batch from the previous *arribada*."

"That's it?" I asked.

"That's all he said of any substance. He claims this shows he'll hatch eighty percent of the eggs he has in the bins here."

He started to add his own commentary but quit when he heard one of the environmentalists grilling Domingo. It seems this fellow had the nerve to question the man's integrity.

Most of the audience could care less. They were standing around ogling the parrot on Jennifer's chest. She was a knock-out in that blouse.

I noticed a lab employee slouching along between the tanks and the wall. He wore dirty green trousers and a long-sleeved shirt. I could swear I'd seen him before; I pointed him out to Teddy. Sure enough. Our first day on the Playa Tortugas, he was the one who absconded with the hatchlings we were shepherding to the sea.

Everyone was leaving. Domingo had evidently decided to keep the show on the road. Casey stood outside talking with the angriest conservationist. Jennifer and I went out to hear what they were saying.

The Mexican was speaking English: "I told him that it is too early to see if his experiment has been a success. What can we tell from these few turtles on display? I am very dissatisfied, *señor*, as I'm sure you are. There is no objectivity here whatsoever."

"I hope those government officials are unhappy, too."

I looked around for Teddy. He'd want to tell what we figured out about the lab employee. Any way I added them up, the implications were nothing but nasty.

Teddy was the last one out. In fact, he had to knock to be let out. The turtle kidnapper, who was locking the door, was pretty surprised he was still in there.

The conservationist had run off to catch up with the others. In a few minutes we could hear the cars roaring off from behind the slaughterhouse. Not even Domingo's friends had wanted to loiter around this place very long.

It was just me and Teddy and Jennifer and Casey. Casey explained to Teddy how the outspoken one was the head of a nationwide organization, and how he wanted to come back to inspect Domingo's rate of success with the lion's share of the eggs.

"Tell him, Teddy," I said.

Teddy pointed to the turtlenapper, who had almost

121

reached the slaughterhouse. "We saw that guy picking up hatchlings on the beach a few days ago."

That disturbed Casey, and then some. "You did?"

I saw my chance for checkmate.

"Yep," I said. "Whenever your friend comes back to inspect this place, Domingo's just going to say, 'Oh, they already hatched and we let 'em go.' "

"You don't think he even has any eggs in those tubs—except the ones he showed us?"

I'd been right the first time about Casey. For all his good intentions he was totally powerless. A typical environmentalist, like my father. If Casey were to write an article about what was happening to the sea turtles, my father would love to read it. He loves to quote environmental disaster trivia. For example, he told me that an amount of the world's rain forest the size of England is slashed and burned every year. Exposed to the sunlight, he said, the tropical soil has all the life-regenerating capacity of a slab of concrete. Trees make oxygen, we breathe oxygen, and so on. That's great that he knows all this stuff—a lot of difference it makes. Before we die from suffocation it's probably going to be nuclear wintertime anyway.

Sorry about the digression. What I should have said was, in my opinion Domingo's bins had about as much chance of sprouting turtles as our flowerbed did ducks, and left it at that.

 25 ≈

ONCE WE LEFT the lab and started north, some kind of breaker tripped in my brain and there was no way to keep Room 837 in the back of my mind any longer. Scenes began to play one after the other in the movie house of my imagination. I have no recall of our walk up the beach, the bus ride into town, or anything that Jennifer or Teddy might have said. I was getting pretty uptight. I wanted so bad not to blow it.

When we got back to the hotel my mother wasn't there. No note or anything. As calm as Jennifer usually stays, she got pretty weirded out. I was hungry, so I talked her into eating in the hotel restaurant. The three of us went through the motions down there. Neither she nor Teddy seemed to have any appetite. I was trying to guess what was best for my purposes and decided I should eat something, not too much or not too little.

Jennifer kept looking to the door as if Mom would walk in. No one said a word. Jennifer fidgeted and Teddy brooded. It seemed like we were under the weight of ten atmospheres. I didn't even try to lighten things up—I had my own concerns.

Finally Jennifer said, "She can't be shopping this long."

"Maybe she left just before we got back," I said.

She knew I didn't believe that. "Something's wrong."

"You can say that again."

It seemed she was about to say something, and she would have if it weren't for Teddy, but she settled for some hard and bitter looks.

Upstairs, we went to our rooms. Teddy sat on his bed with his sea turtle in his lap and petted it mechanically. He was someplace out in the ozone. It was time for me to get ready for my "date."

Maybe it was the lukewarm water, or maybe the anxiety had gotten to me. As I showered, I could care less. It was crazy, I didn't even know her name. For a second I thought about not showing up. Then I knew I was going no matter what. She wouldn't have invited me to her room if she didn't have something in mind, and I needed this more than anything.

When I got out of the shower I stood there awhile staring at my face in the mirror. I sure didn't look like a guy going out for a good time. I needed a boost, that was for sure.

I took the turtle egg out of the sock I'd set on the back of the toilet tank, turned it over and over in my hand, and wondered if I could really eat it. What if it turned out to have a half-formed turtle inside?

There was only one way to find out. I broke it into the glass by the sink. Teddy was right—it was a perfectly fresh egg. In the glass it hardly looked different from a chicken egg.

I held the glass up and looked in the mirror at me holding it. I should have drunk it right away. Then I could have said I didn't know what I was doing, convinced myself I'd had an attack of "temporary depravity." As it was, I looked into my own eyes and recognized all too well that I was about to do the most sordid thing I'd ever done, and I don't mean swallowing a potential sea turtle. I knew I was about to betray my brother.

It's not so hard to betray someone you love. Probably you'll get the chance sometime in your life. When the time comes, it won't be so hard. It's as easy as saying a few words or swallowing an egg. All you have to do is think of yourself first and the rest will come easy.

I stood there with the glass raised as if I were toasting myself. I heard Teddy move across the room and stop right outside the bathroom door. He said in a fragile, hopeful voice, "Travis, do you think Domingo is really hatching any eggs?"

I thought, if I'm going to go for it, I'd better go for it now. So I chugged the egg.

"He's a phony," I said, gagging a bit. I chased the egg with water, then quickly collected the bits of shell, stashed them in the sock, and washed out the glass so nothing would show.

Those were the last words we ever spoke. That egg might have been fresh, but I still can't get the taste of it out of my mouth.

WHEN I GOT OUT of the bathroom, Teddy was back in bed with his turtle, staring into space.

Jennifer stuck her head in the door and said in a no-nonsense tone, "Travis, I'd like to talk with you—in the other room."

"Be right there, Ma'am." I stashed the sock in my suitcase and went right over.

Jennifer noticed I was still wearing only the towel around my waist. "You could have gotten dressed."

"It sounded urgent."

"You weren't serious about leaving."

"You bet I was."

"Where are you going?"

"I'm going out. Did Mom tell us where she was going? Shopping, was that it?"

"Look, Travis, I'm really worried. You can't leave now."

"She's all right," I said sincerely.

"How do you know?"

Now that I'd set her up, she was ripe for a sudden display of ferocity. I exploded. "What do you want me to tell you, the name of the guy she's with?"

"What are you saying?"

"You want the room number? I could find that out for you if you're really interested."

"How do you know?" she asked wildly.

"You don't need to know how I know. Just ask her about 'Mitch' sometime and see what she says. Look, I have to get dressed—I got a date of my own. You just hold the fort."

I wanted to have the last word, so with that I returned to my room.

Teddy wasn't there. His sea turtle was on the nightstand, but Teddy was gone.

I went back to Jennifer's room and told her to look around for him downstairs while I got dressed.

I brushed my teeth, then checked my watch. Thanks to Jennifer I'd gotten behind schedule. I resolved not to let her get to me any more than she already had. I had to keep my head right or I'd blow my big opportunity for sure.

I shaved as deliberately as possible—no nicks even. I slapped on my after-shave, reached for the deodorant. I sang a song to try to soothe myself. Here's how it went:

It's these changes in latitudes, changes in attitudes,
Nothing remains quite the same.

With all of our cunning and all of our running,
If we couldn't laugh we would all go insane.
If we weren't all crazy we would go insane.

Nobody—not Jennifer, Teddy, or my mother—was going to come between me and destiny.

Too much deodorant. It was already a big sticky mess under there, like a washing machine overflowing with suds. I had to clean it out with a washcloth and start over.

I dressed in my best jeans, best shirt, and put on my corduroy jacket. I was ready.

Jennifer came flying in, all overwrought. "I looked all over—he's gone!"

I tried to settle her down by taking a rational tone. "He just wants to say good-bye to his friends, since we're leaving tomorrow."

"He can't go there alone!"

"He's done it before."

"He has?"

"Yep. There's a lot you don't know, eh?"

"Shut up!" she screamed. "There's a lot *you* don't know, Travis, like what's important and what's not! Your little brother's missing in a . . . a foreign country, and you aren't going to do a thing about it! You're the most selfish person I ever met!"

"Hey, calm down!"

"You calm down!"

I felt pretty lame. She'd never skewered me that bad in her life. "Look," I said weakly, "there aren't any muggers around here, or haven't you noticed? This isn't the United States, you know."

"You still aren't going to do anything?"

The steam was still spouting out of her ears.

"I told you. I have a date. You can look for him if you want to, just as well as I can. I'm splitting."

Thinking I'd had the last word, I walked out.

But as I was getting on the elevator she came running down the hallway, all bent out of shape, and yelled "You think you're so different from Mom—you're just like her!"

27

SINCE I WAS TOTALLY broke I had to walk
the length of Punta Blanca all the way to the Strip. I
walked slowly because the night was warm and I didn't
want to arrive at her room all sweaty. The party atmosphere was peaking as the tourists spilled out
of the restaurants into the cobbled streets, but I felt
terrible. I couldn't believe I'd swallowed that egg.
How low could I get? Jennifer was right about me,
and that really hurt. I was spooked about Teddy but
there wasn't anything I was going to do about it.
Every block was taking me farther away from the
Playa Tortugas.

I had all too much time to think. As I went from
Teddy to Jennifer, to my mother, to my father, and
back to Teddy, I knew we were all flying apart. It's

like we were on a wheel spinning faster and faster and we couldn't hold on.

At last I found myself in the elevator at the Oceano Hacienda, pressing the button and heading for the eighth floor. The elevator was making me feel sick. I felt like all my blood had gone to my legs and I'd fall over if I didn't prop myself up.

The doors opened and I walked down the long carpeted hallway. There wasn't a sound. I felt like I was invisible. There it was, Room 837.

I stood in front of the door with my head spinning. I stood there for a long time, more confused than I'd ever been in my life. At last I knocked on the door.

I could hear her coming to the door, and then she was unlatching it, and then we were saying "Hi," and then she was closing the door behind me. She was wearing an embroidered Mexican dress—bright flowers on white muslin—with a healthy scoop down the back. With her dark tan and her loose black hair she was absolutely beautiful in that dress.

"You look great," I said.

"Thanks."

She motioned to the clothes on the bed. "I'm still packing," she said. "Could you get my things off the top shelf in the closet?"

"Sure." I was happy to have something to do.

She had a snorkel, mask, and flippers up there. I brought them out to her and she arranged them in the bottom of her suitcase. There was a chair, and I sat down while she packed. There was something off about the way she moved—she must have hurt herself. When she turned around to talk to me, she couldn't move her neck without moving her whole body. "So what did you do this afternoon?" she asked.

Once again I told her about Teddy. As she folded her clothes I told her about the open market and how I bought the woodcarving for him. I didn't tell her anything about him buying the eggs or our visit to the hatchery.

"You're really very sweet," she said.

Right, I thought bitterly. Mr. Nice Guy. "Did you hurt yourself windsurfing?" I asked.

She smiled with a little grimace. "I pulled a muscle."

How wonderful, I thought. My heart went into overdrive. "Could I give you a neck rub or anything?"

"That would be heavenly," she said. "I would very much like a neck rub. There's some lotion in the bathroom."

Was it fate, or what? I went into the bathroom and the only bottle there, big as life, was the local lotion with the sea-turtle logo. I picked it up and looked at it like this couldn't be happening. Why couldn't anything just be easy?

She sat on the edge of the bed, turned her back to me, and lifted her hair to free her neck and shoulders. I sat beside her and did nothing, just held that bottle in my hand and stared at the sea turtle.

"They say it's the very best thing for your skin," she said.

I squeezed a little onto my palm. It was creamy and smooth and horrifying. After the egg I just couldn't handle this. I felt like I was squeezing the life out of the last turtle on earth.

She turned around from the waist, leaned back,

saw me sitting there staring at the gunk in my hand.

She didn't say anything, and then she said, "I'm sorry. I just didn't think."

"I'm sorry too," I said, and wiped the lotion on my jeans.

I felt like the bottom was dropping out. I had to get to Teddy. I stood up suddenly—I had to get out of there.

"I gotta find my little brother," I said, and I ran off.

28

I BURST THROUGH Jennifer's door yelling, "Where's Teddy?"

Jennifer couldn't tell me. She was sitting on her bed and heaving with sobs. She couldn't even talk.

I ran over and checked our room. Teddy wasn't there. Mom wasn't around either. I felt like I was skydiving without a parachute. My mind was racing and getting nowhere. Somehow all hell had broken loose.

I ran back to Jennifer. "Where's Teddy? Where's Mom?"

She looked up and shook her head back and forth and tried to speak. Nothing would come out but the scary sound of her breathing. Her whole body kept heaving like she was having convulsions. The new blouse with the parrot and flowers was torn from her neckline halfway down to her waist.

"What's going on?" I yelled. That didn't help. She was in a state, like an inconsolable child. I sat down next to her and held her. "What happened, Jennifer?" I asked, as calmly as I could. "Please, Jennifer . . . you can tell me. What happened to your blouse?"

She started crying—that was an improvement. My arms felt like they were paralyzed. I'd never comforted her before that I could think of. I had this feeling I didn't even know my own sister. I couldn't have been doing her much good because I was terrified out of my mind too.

"Please tell me what's going on—did Mom ever get back?"

She shook her head. "Go find Teddy."

"Did you look for him?"

"I tried to," she sobbed.

"What happened?"

She wouldn't say. Her head slumped.

"What happened to your blouse?"

"Find Teddy," she pleaded.

"Not until you tell me what's going on."

"Nothing's going on."

"What happened?"

She looked at me like I wasn't much, but I was all she had. "Bill," she stammered.

I was too scared to be angry. I already knew what I was about to hear.

"He offered me a ride on his motorbike to go find Teddy. When we got up to the top of the hill, he turned around and said we should get to a phone and call for more help."

"Yeah?"

"He took me to where he lives—some shack. He didn't really have a phone."

I knew it. Somewhere at the back of my mind I'd known it all along, what he was up to. The realization only made me sicker. "Then what?"

She hung her head. She was too embarrassed to go on. She was still crying and sniffling.

"Did he—do anything?"

She shook her head.

"Tell me the truth, Jennifer."

"He wanted me to try on a T-shirt—he said it was a present. When I wouldn't, he ripped my blouse. I . . . kicked him as hard as I could, and got away."

What a relief. She was telling the truth. With her, you can tell.

"Good job," I said.

"Hurry, Travis. I'm really scared."

I told her to stay put until Mom or I got back, and I promised her everybody would be okay. Then I flew out of there.

They had to be okay, for my sake.

I ran down the middle of the street among the cars. Three blocks away I found a cab. I tried to think of a word for "emergency." *"Peligroso!"* I yelled frantically. *"Mi hermano!"*

My Spanish vocabulary wasn't exactly coming through for me. I'd just said something to the effect that my brother was dangerous.

"Adónde?" the driver asked.

"Playa Tortugas!" I ordered.

He looked at me suspiciously. Nobody takes a cab there, especially at night. I think he decided I was nuts, and he could do a lot better. Shaking his head, he muttered, *"No es posible."*

I tore out of town on foot. I never ran so hard in my life as I ran up that ridge, down the other side, and onto the beach. The more it hurt the better as far as I was concerned.

I told myself everything was going to turn out okay. The only reason I was so frightened was because of what happened to Jennifer. Teddy would be okay—he knew his way around, the moon was out, he'd done this before. Thank goodness about Jennifer. I lucked out on that one. Maybe I could start acting like a brother for a change. No one could have a better sister than her.

And my mother—I was getting awfully scared about her too. Maybe she took that drive and they had an accident. She'd never know I loved her no matter what. "Some tough guy," she'd said. I wished my father was there. He seemed to be frozen in time back at the airport.

I stayed on the hard-packed sand and out-ran the waves. The way I was running, I thought my heart might give out. Maybe that would even things up on the cosmic scales and let everyone else in the family slide. If one of them was in trouble I'd trade my life for theirs in a minute. What a relief it would be to do something noble for a change. If I went out on a note like that, running to help my brother, I could never blow it afterwards.

Teddy had to be all right. He knew his way around, he'd done it before, I'd never seen anything dangerous around there. So why did I feel sick when I caught sight of the lab glinting in the moonlight?

It's funny the things you think about. When Teddy was three years old he told me he wished he could fly, and I said it was easy for little kids if they knew how. Once you get too big, I explained, you can't fly at all, so if he was serious about it he'd better start right away. He asked me if I would show him how and I said I would.

I told him it was all in the ears. If you warmed up your ears properly it was a cinch to fly. So I'd stand behind him and rub his ears while he concentrated with all his might, and I'd pick up momentum and rub them faster and faster until they turned red and threatened to fall off. Eventually it would hurt too much and he'd have to give up the attempt. How are you ever going to learn to fly, I'd ask, if you never stick with it until you're ready for takeoff?

He was awfully sorry, he'd do better next time.

Never was there a more motivated flying student. He'd tell me how he dreamed every night that he was flying, not fast like Superman, but slowly, as if he were floating. Mom and Dad and Jennifer and I would stand below him, look up, and wave. No one ever spoke, he said, it was just him hovering and us reaching.

He never did learn to fly, and he never blamed me. When he finally gave up, he accepted complete responsibility for his failure.

I knew how I could make that up to him along with a lot of other things. He was always hoping I'd help him scour the hills for king snakes and box turtles. Every day after school he'd set out alone, and since he wouldn't keep the animals he caught, he always came back empty-handed. I never knew what he saw in it.

After this trip I could accompany him, and when the grass dried out in the summer, we could bring along sheets of cardboard from a refrigerator box and toboggan down the hillsides. . . .

Up ahead of me, at the end of the line of poles that made up the near side of the turtle stockade, a figure still as a statue stood holding something in the moonlight. As I neared with lungs bursting I saw it was Casey, with Teddy splayed unnaturally in his arms.

It was written in Casey's face, it was written in Teddy's dangling arms and legs and the way his head slumped against Casey's chest, but I couldn't see it because I wouldn't have it and if I wouldn't accept it then it couldn't be true. "What's the matter with him?" I demanded.

Casey said softly, "Travis, he's dead."

What did Casey know? Teddy was *my* brother. "Give him to me!"

I took him from Casey. He was heavy and cold. My own breath was still heaving in and out of me in huge gasps. I'd give him mine, I could save him with my breath.

I laid him down on the beach, tilted his head back, pinched his nose, and breathed quick breaths into him. His chest rose, the air was getting through. I pumped with my doubled fist on his breastbone, ten, twelve times. How many were you supposed to?—I couldn't remember. I breathed into him again. He wasn't responding. Was I doing it right? I was so full of fear I couldn't think at all. I had to do it right, I had to bring him back. My brother, my only brother. Teddy, please don't die. I love you, I love you. Don't you hear me? I love you!

I was shouting, I guess. Casey knelt beside me as I pumped on Teddy's chest again, and he said gently, "I tried that a long time already, Travis."

"So what?" I screamed.

"Well let me help you, then."

Casey checked Teddy's throat for a pulse and took over the breathing.

"He can't die," I bawled. "He's only nine years old."

"I found him face down with a turtle pinned under him."

"What do you mean, a turtle?"

"A live, adult sea turtle. All I can figure is, he was freeing those turtles in there."

He'd nodded toward the turtle stockade. "Sounds like him," I said with a desperate laugh.

"They're really too heavy for him to carry, but I guess he was."

I turned on Casey. "So what! What happened to him?"

"I don't know what it was, but I don't think he drowned."

He checked the artery on the side of Teddy's throat again, then looked at me full of pity. "Travis, there's no pulse at all."

"Get away!"

Casey stood up and backed away a few steps. I continued furiously, I don't know how long. Eventually I had to give up. I pulled Teddy into my arms and against my chest. I kissed his sandy cheek. I kissed his hair. He was dead, dead, dead. And I was alive.

≈ 29

CASEY SAID we had to call the police. He said there was a phone in the lab—he'd break in through a window. He told me to stay right where I was and assured me he wasn't going farther than the lab. I didn't care where he went or who he called. He needn't have worried about me going anywhere. I wasn't going to run off on my brother ever again.

It felt like Casey was gone a long time. He definitely got inside, because the lights came on. I sat there and stared at all the small footprints between me and the water, going in both directions. They were Teddy's. I knew what they meant: he had carried any number of turtles from the pen, around the poles, to the sea. Of course that's what he would have done—that's who he was. I could see him staggering under their weight.

If I'd cared about him for two seconds, back when Jennifer was begging me to, I would have figured out what he knew he had to do. Nobody knew him better than me.

The tide was rising and each little wave that ran up the beach erased a few more of his footsteps, and there was nothing I could do about it.

Casey came back with a strange expression on his face, and he said, "The door wasn't locked. The only thing I can think is, he must have unlatched a window this afternoon. He was the last one out, wasn't he?"

I couldn't speak. I was remembering how he had to knock to be let out.

"He dug in the sand in the tubs here and there all over the lab. You know what—there weren't any eggs."

"Surprise," I said bitterly.

"You were right this afternoon."

"And Teddy had to find out if I was."

He nodded cautiously. "You know what else—the hatchlings in those tanks were gone, every one."

"He let them go."

"And then he decided to free the adults in the pen. Travis, I think your brother's the most remarkable person I ever met."

"I know," I said. "I know."

I broke down crying right in front of him. The shock was wearing off, and I felt the grief pour in and take hold of every fiber in me. If I'd cut off my leg with a chain saw I could have endured it better than this. I flipped out. I ran down the beach screaming. I threw myself down. Casey tried to help me. I can't remember anything he said or anything I said. Finally he restrained me. Somewhere in there the police showed up. I remember seeing Domingo's face. There were soldiers, too, with big rifles.

The next thing I can recall, Mom and Jennifer came rushing across the beach toward all these people standing around. They didn't have any idea what was going on, and then they found out.

My mother started screaming. There's nothing more frightening than a grown woman grieving at the top of her lungs. She had a deep cut in her forehead and it started bleeding all over her and Teddy. Jennifer was doubled up in the sand moaning and sobbing.

An army truck drove out on the beach and they put Teddy's body on a stretcher. How I wished it was me.

 30

JENNIFER CALLED Dad from the hospital and told him. She was the only one who could do it. Afterwards all she said was, "He's going to come as fast as he can."

My mother looked dreadful with fourteen stitches in her forehead. The police called a cab for us. On the way back to the Sol Mar none of us spoke, not a word. No weeping, no gnashing of teeth. We were zombies.

They went to their room and I went to mine. Everything of Teddy's, of course, was just as he left it. Through the wall I heard Jennifer and Mom weeping. I sat on my bed and stared at the sea turtle and the frog side-by-side on the nightstand. Somehow they said it all. I pulled the frog off his pedestal and tore him limb from limb. Then I crushed the pieces in my hands and shredded them into crumbs.

I turned out the light, collapsed on my bed, and started picturing Teddy alive, not dead. I saw him digging furiously in the sand; I saw him standing big-eyed in the market as I gave him the carving; I saw us swimming with the turtles. I cried until I fell asleep, and then I saw him again in my dreams. I can remember the gist of it because I've dreamt countless variations of that dream since the first night. He's in danger for his life and I could save him if only I could reach him, but my legs won't work. I take a few steps, they turn to rubber, and I fall down over and over and over again.

We received a message in the afternoon that the autopsy report was ready at the coroner's office in the city morgue. Also that we should bring clothes for Teddy. Just after that my father showed up, looking pretty haggard. He didn't burst in asking what happened, he just cried when he saw us and hugged us one at a time. I couldn't look in his face, I was so ashamed. Mom mumbled something incoherent when he asked her how she cut her forehead. Jennifer gave him the message from the coroner and Dad said we should all go down there together.

I let Jennifer slide in next to Mom in the back of the taxi. The less I had to look at my mother's face the better. Dad rode in front with the driver. My mother's hands were clasped tightly atop Teddy's clothes in her lap. I held his ironwood turtle in mine. Both of us needed something of his to cling to.

The taxi wound so deliberately through the cobbled streets, I could feel every stone under the wheels. The driver must have noticed we weren't out for a joyride. Come to think of it, my father had told him where we were going.

Halfway across town Dad turned around as if he were going to say something, but he didn't. Jennifer felt sorry for him and said, "You must be exhausted, Dad, traveling all night."

"I'm all right. But how are all of you? I don't hear a word."

None of us could answer him.

"Jennifer said on the phone that Teddy was rescuing turtles or something, that's all. Who was with him?"

I saw Jennifer bite her lip.

"*No one* was with him," I said.

Surprised and confused, he looked to each of us to see if someone would explain. Mom broke out weeping.

My father looked right at me and his face crumpled as he said, "I wasn't there either, Travis. I was thousands of miles away."

The coroner spoke fluent English and greeted us in funereal tones as the four of us filed into his office and sank into plush, oversized armchairs. He noticed the woodcarving but he didn't say anything about it. A kind and dignified man with gray in his hair, he wore a dark suit and kept the pictures of his family in large individual frames propped up on the immaculately groomed surface of his desk. He had five lovely children, a handsome wife, and an electric pencil sharpener. He told us that Teddy died of an "aneurism."

I'd heard that word before but I had no idea what it meant. Before he could explain there came a soft knock at the door, and a younger man came in and spoke in Spanish to the coroner. The coroner asked my mother, "May we have the clothes you brought, please." She stood up and handed them to the assistant. A white sock fell off the folded clothes to the floor. That sock falling was about the saddest thing I've ever seen, I don't know why. I reached and picked it up and gave it to the man. *"Gracias,"* he said to me, and then whispered something to the coroner.

"Are there shoes?" the coroner asked.

My mother went blank, she just stood there with her mouth open. Jennifer answered for her. She was almost as rattled. "No, we forgot his shoes," she said, as if they were supremely important.

The coroner could see Mom couldn't cope, so he asked Dad, "Do you wish—"

Dad shook his head and said quietly, "He doesn't need shoes."

"Very well."

The assistant left and the coroner selected a pencil from a circular pencil-stand full of them. All of them were full-length and finely sharpened. He seemed to be inspecting the pencil for imperfections as he began to speak. "Let me try to explain the findings of the autopsy as simply as possible. There was a weakness in one of the three layers of the wall of one of the arteries that supply the brain with blood. The weakness has existed since birth. When there is such a weakness there exists the possibility that the blood pressure in the skull will rise to the extent that the wall of the artery cannot withstand it, and forms what looks like a small balloon."

"The aneurism?" asked Dad.

"Exactly. And if the balloon bursts, as it did in your son's case, the result is a massive intracranial hemorrhage, and very often sudden death."

"He didn't suffer? . . ."

"No, I can assure you. He died quite suddenly."

Then the coroner paused, and said to all of us, "I wish to express my deepest sympathy. Unless you have any further questions . . ."

I did. He wasn't going to let me off that easy. There had to be more to it and I had to know. "How'd he get this weakness in that artery?"

"He was born with it—but let me assure you that doesn't mean that any of the rest of you have the same thing."

"Does this mean," my father suggested almost hopefully, "this was . . . bound to happen sooner or later?"

The coroner was growing uncomfortable. "Not necessarily . . ." he said cautiously.

"What do you mean, 'not necessarily'?" I insisted.

"Millions of people have these weak spots in their arteries and go through their whole lives never knowing it, without an aneurism ever developing."

There. Teddy could have lived to be ninety.

"So it's really rare to die from these things," I said.

"No, it's quite common. It's more . . . rare . . . in children, but more common than you might think."

Mom and Jennifer weren't saying anything, but they were listening to every word.

Dad leaned forward onto the edge of his chair. "If the aneurism bursts, is it always . . . fatal, and can the weaknesses be detected beforehand?"

"The answer to your first question is no. Some people survive the incident, but often suffer paralysis or brain damage in different degrees. As to detection of weak spots—potential aneurisms—yes, that is just beginning, but correction is rarely undertaken—"

"Because it's a drastic procedure and there'll probably never be a problem."

My father seemed somewhat relieved, but there was something I had to know. "So he just happened to die when he did—it would have been just as likely any other time, like in his sleep?"

That really made the coroner squirm, and I saw he knew something, but he'd been trying to let us off the hook. As he paused and groped for words, I got more specific. "Did it have anything to do with carrying those turtles?"

He started slowly, looking at me, like "If you insist." He said, "The aneurism is more likely to develop with increased blood pressure, yes."

"And carrying those turtles increased his blood pressure?"

"Dramatically, of course. He was repeatedly carrying his own body weight, as I understand it."

That's what I'd been trying to dig out. Hauling around those turtles killed him. Wasn't that obvious all along? And there's no way I would have let him do that if I were there with him. Maybe I would have carried them for him—after all, we'd rescued those box turtles together.

The coroner tried to rescue some dignity for the occasion. "Quite a remarkable feat your brother performed."

There was that word "remarkable" again.

He walked over to my chair and put a hand on my shoulder. Probably he was wrong, but he thought I was taking this the hardest. "People in your brother's situation are living at risk every day of their lives without even knowing it. You mustn't blame yourselves that the call for him came at an early age."

I eyeballed him and said, "There wasn't any 'call.' "

"Then you might at least consider that he died in a noble and courageous manner. Very few human beings are that fortunate."

I'd have to think about that one—Teddy being fortunate. I'd be able to run a little ways with it. He wouldn't live to see the sea turtles wiped out, along with most of the other species of wild animals on the earth. He wouldn't live to see the planet paved, and he'd miss the biggest fireworks show of all time at the end.

The assistant rapped softly on the door again. Through the clouded glass he looked like he was in a horror movie. He stood back—apparently he wasn't coming in. The coroner said to all of us, "You may go in now," and to Dad, "Will you be opening the casket at home?"

Obviously Dad hadn't thought about any of that, but he appeared to make up his mind. "No . . . I don't think so."

The coroner showed us out the door and gave us to his assistant. He said to us, "*Vaya con Dios,* my friends."

The man led us down the hallway to an unmarked door, which he unlocked and stood solemnly beside. It was all happening too fast. I hadn't known we were going to see Teddy's body at all. We looked to each other uncertainly and Dad said, "Let's go in together, and say our last good-byes."

We walked into the room. It was large and had nothing at all in it except a casket with the lid up set on a stand in the middle, and some folding chairs along one wall. We stalled out right by the door, but Dad encouraged us forward and we kept going. Mom and Jennifer were starting to cry and I did my best to hang on, but I only lasted until we got close enough and Teddy came into view. All the sun he'd gotten made him look too healthy to be dead. We all broke down.

Dad pulled himself together, walked up close, stood quietly a long time, then kissed Teddy on the cheek. I heard him say, "Good-bye, Son. We love you, we'll never forget you." When he stepped back I saw the tears streaming down his face.

Jennifer was next. She went up sobbing, kissed Teddy, and said, "You were so good. You could never hurt anyone. Good-bye, Teddy, I love you."

I looked at my mother. She wasn't going anywhere. She was heaving with barely suppressed hysteria, and Dad went to her to hold her up.

My turn. I stepped forward and looked down into his face, his peaceful, unsmiling, beautiful face. I thought, I love you brother, I love you with all my heart.

I had to speak to him, I had to tell him something. Tell him what? I felt like my grandfather must have, trapped without speech by his breathing machine. Then I felt the turtle-carving in my hands, and I reached out and lifted his folded hands, and slipped the turtle a little ways under them.

"I love you, Paco," I sobbed. "Are you navigating by the stars?"

31

WE WAITED OUT in front of the morgue while my father talked with the coroner some more. When he emerged from the building he had a determined look on his face, and it was apparent he meant to take charge and inspire some confidence in the troops. As if it were good news, he said he'd contacted the authorities who would be in charge of releasing Teddy's body, and that it looked like we could go home the next day if he hurried to their offices this afternoon.

He took us back to the hotel and told us to stay there while he took care of the paperwork. He said we'd have dinner as soon as he got back, and then he made a speech about how we all had a lot to talk about but we didn't have to talk tonight, and the best thing for all of us would be to get home as soon as possible, rest up, and then we could begin to put our lives back together.

Thinking that speech would hold us, he ran down the hall to the elevator. Big mistake. Had he forgotten? We weren't exactly a cohesive bunch. We could fly off as easy as he just had. Besides, we'd been practicing at it all week.

Take me, for instance. He hadn't been gone five minutes before I slipped out. There was a place I had to go and something I had to do.

I stood on the edge of that flat boulder where Teddy sat less than forty-eight hours before and told me what it felt like to be a turtle. I looked straight down into the surf slamming the granite hundreds of feet below and I worked up all the self-hate I could muster, which was considerable. It's my fault, I told myself. It's my fault, it's all my fault. Teddy would be alive if I had stayed with him, I know it.

My heart raced—I was moments away from taking that one step forward.

They say that when you're about to die your whole life passes before you. That's not what I saw. I saw people, I saw faces. I saw Teddy's face up close with his blue eyes and white-blond hair, and he was smiling.

What would Teddy think? Now he was grinning. He thought it was the stupidest thing he ever heard. Cheeseball yourself!

I saw Jennifer's face. She's telling me this will be the ultimate selfishness.

I saw my parents' faces searching for me with eyes full of love and immeasurable sadness. My mother, so much like me.

Teddy's asking, "Who would care for the turtles?"

I realized I was bargaining with myself. I'm the one I have to answer to after everything.

I'd seen what I could do, for Teddy and for me: live for both of us.

And if there was going to be any room for him, there were going to have to be some changes.

≈ 32

HURRYING BACK, I resolved to try to be of some help. I don't know why I expected the three of them to freeze while I went to the edge and back, but I had. It came as a big surprise to find Jennifer alone and nearly unglued.

"Travis!" she wailed. "Where have you been?"

"I . . . was airing out my head."

"Mom's gone! And I should have known—she was talking crazy! She shouldn't be alone, Travis—there's no telling what she might do!"

Sure, I could see it now. She and I had to be going through the same hell.

"What'd she say?"

"She said Teddy was her soul, she didn't have one of her own."

"What else?"

"Nothing that made any sense."

"Where's Dad?"

"He's out looking for her. But I didn't know where to tell him to look!"

Jennifer started crying. "I thought she went to sleep, so I took a shower. When I came out she was gone! I should never have—"

"Let me think! Where would she be!"

"Don't you know something about where she's been going?"

"Sure, but why would she go there?"

"How do I know?—hurry, if you're going."

Maybe she would go to him. Maybe she needed Mitch to comfort her—who knows?

"Give me some money for a cab!"

She quickly produced the last of her pesos.

"If she's there I'll find her and bring her back, don't worry. You stay here and don't do anything crazy yourself, okay?"

When I got to the Sheraton, all I had to go on was the name "Mitch." Fortunately, there was only one Mitchell staying at the hotel.

The room was on the top floor. Standing at the door to Mr. Big Bucks' suite, I froze up. There was no way I wanted to actually meet him face-to-face, yet I had to find my mother.

I listened, couldn't hear a thing. I swallowed the lump in my throat and knocked at the door. No answer. I knocked again, louder—still no answer. I was about to give up when I tried the door and found it unlocked. I opened it, half-expecting the worst.

The place was huge, sumptuous, a bona fide penthouse. It seemed empty, like it was in-between guests. I walked around the bed and was startled to find someone in the room after all. On the floor, huddled up against the wall, was my mother. She was hugging her knees to her chest, rocking, and staring out the open balcony doors toward the sea. She had those nasty-looking stitches in her head.

I looked around for Mitch in another bedroom and the bathrooms. Not one sign of him, not even a toothbrush. I walked past my mother's line of sight a couple of times and she didn't even blink.

"Where is he?" I demanded.

No answer. No expression. She just kept rocking.

"Everyone's looking for you. Jennifer's scared something happened to you."

She put her head down on her knees. She looked like a frail little girl all curled up like that.

"Do something," I screamed. "You can't just sit there like that. You can't hide from us."

My voice was cracking and getting shrill, and I just couldn't stop. "Answer me! Is this your plan? Stay here forever? What about us?"

The wilder I got the farther away she retreated, like she was disappearing into herself and making her big escape into permanent unreality. I couldn't even hear her breathing.

"Oh, no you don't," I said fiercely. "It's not that easy!" I grabbed her by the shoulders and shook her.

Nothing.

I shook her again, harder. Before I could stop myself I slapped her and shook her and slapped her again. She gasped so sharply I stopped, scared by what I had done.

"Leave me alone!" she screamed. "Leave me alone."

Then she started crying, I mean really crying, in huge choking sobs. I thought she was going to explode. Now I wanted to help her but couldn't. This was getting out of hand.

She was hyperventilating—I had to calm her down. I talked to her. I kept talking to her all the while. I was so pumped up I can't remember much of what I said, but I know I told her "Everything's going to be all right" at least a few dozen times. I didn't believe it myself, and I sounded so scared I'm sure I wasn't very convincing.

After some time I coaxed her up and across the room to an armchair. I grabbed a box of tissues for her, and she blew her nose and wiped her eyes. "How'd you find me?" she asked.

"I saw you with him. . . ."

Then she started crying again, and whimpered, "I'm no mother." She put her head down in her hands and wept.

She cried like she was never going to stop, until I knelt by her and said, "I was no kind of brother."

She looked up sharply. "He worshipped you, Travis—don't blame yourself. It was all my fault."

"No, that's not true, Mom. I ran off on him, and I knew what I was doing."

"It wasn't the same—"

I had to tell her. No matter how hard it was, I had to summon the guts to tell her.

"It was the same. I could have gone right after him. I went to see a woman I met."

She waved me off. She wanted all the blame for herself.

"Look, Mom, I almost jumped off a cliff an hour ago. Do you hear what I'm saying?"

She looked at me like she was seeing me dead. She realized she'd almost lost both of her sons.

I was approaching overload, and started to cry myself. "Don't you want to know why I didn't jump?—I figured out I was only thinking of myself. So are you Mom, so are you!"

She looked at me differently than she ever had before. She wasn't exactly my mother, she was just a person.

"We're both into 'me first,' Mom, looking for the easy way out. What about Jennifer and Dad?"

"What can I do, Travis, I have nowhere to turn!"

"Come back!"

"Your father could never forgive me."

"He would. They'd forgive both of us."

She anguished over that for a long time, then whispered, "Do you think so, Travis? Do you really think so?"

"It wouldn't be easy, but nothing's ever going to be easy."

Suddenly her eyes were pleading with me, desperate and compelling. "No one would ever believe me, but I broke it off with—that man—before Teddy died, Travis. I was going to go with the three of you but instead I went to tell him it was over—I'd been miserable all week. He insisted we go on the drive and talk it over, and we went to a village in the mountains, but on the way back we ran over a dead horse in the road and wrecked the car . . ."

160

She was talking so fast, she had to stop for air, and burst out crying again.

"That's how you got the cut."

"Yes. It took forever to get back. He caught a flight out—he doesn't even know what's happened."

"And he left you the room?"

She winced. "He said I might need a place to 'unwind.' I guess that's what I've been doing—unwinding."

"Tell Dad. Tell him what you just told me."

"You know when I knew I couldn't leave my family, Travis? . . . It was at the market, when you gave that carving of the turtle to Teddy. The two of you—"

She cried, and I cried with her. We held on to each other and cried. Suddenly there was no stopping our grief, and we let it all out. All those years we spent maneuvering for position were gone. We needed each other now. I guess we always had, but now we knew it. It was Teddy who brought us to terms.

We went back to the Sol Mar together. It turned out to be horribly painful for all of us, an operation on our souls without the benefit of anesthetic, but in the end there was enough forgiveness to go around.

≈ 33

HERE WAS SOMETHING I had to do for myself before we left Punta Blanca.

About midnight, I walked to the Playa Tortugas. The moon was several days past full, but plenty bright. No one was on the beach. I found the spot where Teddy had planted the eggs and I said a prayer. Then I continued on to the stockade.

All night I freed turtles. My heart was big enough and my back was strong enough to carry the load. One by one I carried them in Teddy's footsteps around the poles to the sea. The sun was rising as the last one trudged forward, gained deeper water, and disappeared.

WILL HOBBS is the author of four books for young people including the popular *Bearstone*. He lives in Durango, Colorado with his wife Jean.